— THE —
FISH HOUSE
GANG

— THE —
FISH HOUSE GANG

KENNETH L. FUNDERBURK

ARCHWAY
PUBLISHING

Archway Publishing books may be ordered through booksellers or by contacting:

Archway Publishing
1663 Liberty Drive
Bloomington, IN 47403
www.archwaypublishing.com
1-(888)-242-5904

ISBN: 978-1-4808-0074-8 (sc)
ISBN: 978-1-4808-0075-5 (e)

Library of Congress Control Number: 2013907256

Printed in the United States of America

Archway Publishing rev. date: 4/26/2013

— 1 —

A murky, pink twilight bathed the men in an eerie glow, which would leave any onlooker with a palpable sense of being in the presence of evil. And so it was that evil became incarnate in this group of common thugs.

Randall Moss came upon the idea of robbing a man he knew had plenty of cash on hand, but he needed some help. His plan began to solidify when a drug dealer from Texas contacted him, wanting to hire him to kill the very man he intended to rob. He could not believe his good fortune when he was paid twenty-five thousand dollars in advance and was to get twenty-five thousand more when he completed the job. Now he would really be in high cotton. Next time he boasted about being a hired killer, it would be true. When he put the group together, they would never know this part of the plan.

He had quickly gathered three of his friends and acquaintances, plus his father, Matt Moss, all of whom were now in his back yard drinking beer and plotting a quick military operation to relieve Thomas Reed of the money stored in his safe. Others would become involved in the plot. The housekeeper, who was the girlfriend of one of the group, was crucial to the operation. Her job was to disable the security system.

Randall lived in downtown Fort Walton Beach, a few blocks on the west side of Eglin Parkway. This was definitely not the pretty part of Fort Walton, but a run down, crime infested area. The back yard had an old barbecue grill and a big live oak tree for shade. It was a fitting venue for the evil which was being planned by the Ninja gang this evening. Crime was an old friend in this back yard.

Randall Moss was known as a loud-mouth braggart whose great accomplishment in life was his failed career as a karate instructor. His big dream was to become a famous hit man. Given a little liquor and an audience,

Randall would brag about his fictitious exploits as a hit man and the amount of money he had made in this line of work. Among his drinking buddies, however, Randall was known as a spaced-out petty crook who would steal your gold teeth if you let him.

At five feet eleven inches tall and two hundred pounds, some athletic ability and martial arts training, Randall could qualify as a tough guy. With the character of an alley cat, he leaned more toward the description of a bona fide bad-ass. Randall could be a good man to have on your side in a bar fight. Randall's problem was that more often than not he would have started the fight and have you sucked into the melee simply to defend yourself.

Randall had managed to accumulate a cast of characters around him from his failed karate studio. Their intelligence and character made Randall seem, by comparison, a worthy leader. Chuck, Barney and Floyd were the collective halfwits from the karate class who believed that drinking beer with Randall was an accomplishment in life. When Randall asked them to be his partners in the ninja robbery, they literally became starry-eyed with anticipation. The deal was simply too good to pass up.

Only Randall's father, Matt, had enough sense and experience to understand the dangers involved. This robbery was not Matt's first rodeo. Matt had lived his life on the edge just like his father and uncles. He knew what prison life was like. He knew his son, Randall, had not fallen far from the tree. Matt was here to keep his son from doing something totally stupid, like killing Mr. Reed or anyone else in the house. Matt had the fleeting thought that had his own father kept him in check as a youth, perhaps his life and Randall's life would have been different. That thought was quickly snuffed out by the long shadow of family history of crime and violence. The die was cast in stone.

Then there was a real estate lady, Gertrude Wade, who would provide the escape vehicle and the place to stage the operation. Although Gertrude was married, her sexual exploits and shady dealings were well known in certain circles of Fort Walton, Florida. She and Randall were known to be involved in sport sex with each other. The depth of her involvement with the details of the robbery was unknown, but those who knew her recognized her ability to sniff out the money.

Randall had worked for Thomas Reed at one of his used car lots, which was more of a front for drug trafficking than a business. Randall worked long enough with Reed to be able to identify his Mexican contacts. Randall kept his eyes and ears open enough to detect a pattern in the times when Reed would be flush with cash. He determined that Reed was part of a Mexican drug cartel and believed Reed was skimming money from the Mexicans. Randall figured that Reed's friends had actually put the contract on him for stealing money or not paying for product he had purchased. The Mexicans, of course, had other motives. This wasn't information Randall planned to disclose to his group of thugs. Neither did he disclose the robbery to his employers who were paying him the twenty-five thousand up front.

"Son," said the elder Matt Moss, "we ain't gonna have no gunplay on this caper, are we?" I'll drive the van and go in the house, but I don't want anybody gettin' shot." Matt took a big sip of his Bud, a big draw on his cigar, blew out the smoke, gave Randall the evil eye and snarled, "Now boys, listen up. No gunplay. That goes for all you boys here in this yard."

"Papa," said Randall, "I got this covered. You know we've got this thing planned to a T. We got enough guys to be in and out in less than thirty minutes with the safe. The security cameras are gonna be off. They'll all have masks and gloves and be dressed in black. Thomas and Delores Reed won't be a problem for me to tie up using my martial arts training. Quit worrying."

"Yes, but what about all those kids they've got in that mansion? I've heard they have about six or seven," said Barney.

"Don't worry about that," said Randall. "They're all disabled kids. They don't know nothing. The maid said they keep them drugged up pretty good. They won't be able to interfere with us and won't remember anything.

"Does everybody have their assignments and know what they're supposed to do?

"We'll meet back here at three p.m. tomorrow. The ninja outfits, gloves and masks are in. I don't want any skin showing and no talking. I'll do the talking. We've practiced this several times, so there's no excuse for screwing up."

Randall pointed to Chuck, a big guy at six feet and two hundred fifty pounds, a bald head with a moon shaped face. He looked like a bar room regular, which he was. Chuck was a man of few words and a passive personality. His demeanor tended to cover his deep seated anger at the world which boiled just below the surface, waiting for an excuse to explode. Chuck was Randall's right hand man and was the team leader.

"Chuck, you got the team ready to take out the safe and all the equipment you need, I hope?" asked Randall.

"Yes, sir," said Chuck. "We know where the safe is. While you're securing the Reeds, we'll have that safe loaded up and ready to roll."

Floyd asked, "How much money you think's in that safe?"

At twenty years of age, Floyd was the youngest man on the team. He considered himself above the law. If it felt good, he had a god-given right to indulge himself. Floyd was the talker in the group. With a slim frame and at five feet six inches tall, he wasn't going to scare anyone. Floyd fit in as the gofer and the court jester.

Randall looked at Floyd and replied, "Don't you worry about that, son. There's going to be more than enough to take care of your sorry ass," explained Randall. "You just make sure you put your full weight behind that safe and get it in that van as fast as you can."

Randall continued, "Now, Barney, you get that door opened fast. It shouldn't be locked, but if it is, use that ramming rod. We don't need to waste a lot of time getting in. Nobody can see us from the road, but we don't want Reed to have time to defend himself."

"Randall," said Barney, "that door will be opened by the time you get there from the truck. Reed won't know what hit him."

Barney was a simple minded country boy. He was medium height and medium built, but he learned how to work hard on the farm. His normal dress was blue jeans, tee shirt and an Alabama baseball cap. He usually needed a shave and his brown hair stuck out in all directions from under the baseball cap. What money he was able to earn was from part time work at veterinarian clinics. He was good with animals. His strong suit was that Randall could depend on him to follow instruction. Barney was responsible for cooking the barbecue and icing down the beer for their back yard planning session. The ninja must have been pleased with his cooking judged by the way they consumed all the barbecue.

Barney surveyed the scene and had that feeling that all was well in the world this night.

"Now, boys, I don't want any of you showing up here tomorrow drunk.

Drink what you want tonight, but tomorrow, no booze and no weed," commanded Randall. "Let's go through a dry run or two and then I got to get out of here and pick up the van from Gertrude."

"Hey, Randall," said Floyd, "don't you want me to come along and help you service that sweet thing?"

Randall said, "You'd have to take a bath and get your teeth fixed first. But don't you worry; I can handle it and if I do need help, I'll call in some rich dudes she and I can fleece."

Floyd said, "After this heist, how about using me? I'll have some money then."

"Don't give me any ideas, Floyd," said Randall.

"Hell," said Floyd, "that girl looks so good it might be worth a fleecing to get some of her ass!"

Randall turned to Floyd and told him to "cut the shit." "Now gather around boys, we've got work to do."

Once Randall got their attention, he gave his best first sergeant dressing down to the men. He then talked through each phase of the plan. He made each man carefully recite their part of the plan. He especially centered on Barney and had him go through his preparations with his girl friend, who was Reed's maid, about how and when to disable Reed's security cameras. After two hours of grilling the men, he pronounced them ready.

"Okay men, I believe you are ready," said Randall. "The party's over. Finish up your beer, let's clean up the place, then get your asses home and rest up for tomorrow."

— 2 —

At the same time Chic viewed the concert hall from backstage, waiting for the music to begin, the group of friends who had gathered in Fort Walton to drink beer in the back yard of Randall Moss and plan the robbery dispersed to rest up for the event.

The crowd of well-dressed patrons began to arrive early at the Bill Heard Theater on Broad Street in Columbus, Georgia, excited about the performance of Mendelssohn's *Elijah*. This was a special event that combined the Columbus Symphony Orchestra, the Columbus State University Choral Union and visiting soloists, one of whom was a popular tenor, Charles (Chic) Sparks.

Chic was a practicing clinical psychologist in Fort Walton Beach, Florida, specializing in eating disorders and addictive personality disorders in his own clinic. He was a part-time voice coach at Pensacola Christian College in Pensacola, Florida and served as a profile consultant to various police departments in the Florida Panhandle.

Music was Chic's first love, but the necessities of life dictated another field as the source of his income. Chic started out in music at Florida State. He realized that music was too non-lucrative to support a man and his family, though his talent did keep him in demand as a tenor soloist for special events. He changed his major to criminal justice, where he hoped to earn a stable living. After serving the country as a Ranger at Fort Benning, Georgia, Chic became a detective in the homicide division on the Tallahassee police force. He continued his education and finally got his doctorate degree in psychology at Florida State.

Chic's knowledge of police procedures and his reputation in the law enforcement community in the Panhandle area enabled him to act as advisor to sheriff and police departments, particularly in the area of profiling in white-collar crime. It was in this capacity that his good friend, Chief Detective Heath Moore, would eventually call Chic in for consultation in the murder of Gertrude and other related issues.

This was not Chic's first trip to Columbus, Georgia. He had come through Fort Benning to train at the ranger school and had performed at the Bill Heard Theater on other occasions. The Schwob School of Music, which was part of Columbus State University, was physically attached to the Bill Heard Theatre.

The Schwob School of Music had gained a grand reputation as a leading music conservatory in the Southeast. The facility was one of a kind on a grand scale, usually seen only in large metropolitan areas, certainly not in a midsize town like Columbus, Georgia. Columbus was distinctively blessed with the Springer State Theater and a history of great musicians and outstanding vocal artists who brought these grand facilities to life. This unique venue was a favorite of many performing artists and rated high on Chic's list of great places to sing.

Chic was always a crowd favorite. The joy in his voice as he sang was contagious. One couldn't hear him sing without the soul spontaneously joining in with a symphonic melody. The music buffs were there for Mendelssohn, but the buzz of excitement was for Chic.

The excitement in the audience always built when Chic took the stage. Chic often felt that as he sang angels came down from heaven and lit up his soul and the countenance of the crowd was magically transformed. The energy of the crowd fed back to him, producing a special zone that only a performer could know. Coming to the stage, waiting for that moment when the orchestra reached the entrance point and with a tone that one believed pleased God and man, Chic acknowledged a gift from God. He saw a disparate group of people coalesce at a place of joy. At this moment of exhilaration, Chic felt that heaven must be largely composed of singing choirs of angels praising God. The experience, while totally physical, became mystical, magical and beyond verbal expression. It was that private zone relived in one's dream world—that time at night when the soul is in wonderment and can experience the universe unfettered, free of time and distance.

Man has always been transformed by music, but when mixed with a crowd at a live performance, there is a magic that morphs the people into a tangible force greater than the sum of its parts. Every crowd thus afflicted reveals a different personality.

As Chic warmed up backstage, his mind wandered through these thoughts and pondered what this crowd would be like. Happy, tentative, slow to applaud, excited, involved, pensive—who knows? The amazing part was that the crowd never saw the personality that it mysteriously emanated to an onlooker. The experience always amazed Chic. How was it possible for a group of people who are strangers to suddenly take on a distinct hue, color and persona?

The time was fast approaching for the soloist to enter the stage. The choir was working its way into position. The orchestra was tuning to the A note and the crowd was quickly taking their seats. Standing in the wing, waiting, Chic thought of the absurdity of his world. In this forum, he felt like he was in a holy place about to join many others in making music in harmony with the angels in heaven. However, in his everyday work as a clinical psychologist, he knew that he was dealing with the beastly nature of man, which could be evil and dark. If left unchecked, the dark forces of man's nature would devour every good thing in man's soul.

Then there was his work he often did with the police departments, profiling and devising schemes to formulate ways to proceed with investigations. Here, man as beast was in his full glory.

As Chic prepared his mind for *Elijah*, this juxtaposition of good versus evil propelled him to the stage, ready to slay evil with tools provided by God and Mendelssohn. The crowd was not disappointed with the results.

— 3 —

Randall Moss awoke the next morning with a hangover, a sore pelvis bone and the scent of Gertrude's perfume. It was another beautiful, cloudless day in Fort Walton Beach, Florida. When he finally got his eyes focused and looked out his bedroom window at the beautiful day, he thought of what a beautiful day it was to whack that bastard Reed. The mocking bird singing outside the window lifted his spirits on the great prospects this day held. *Perhaps,* he reasoned*, the gods are truly with me today! Nothing can go wrong.* And so it is that God allows the sun to shine on the good and bad alike. At three p.m., the group of thugs arrived at Randall's back yard in Fort Walton.

"Listen up," instructed Randall. "Line up for inspection. Does everybody have equipment and ninja outfits ready?"

Chuck answered, "Yes, sir. All equipment is in place and we all have our outfits ready to put on."

"When we get there, I'll do the talking. The rest of you keep quiet," said Randall. "This operation is to come off like we're trained professionals or I'll kick your asses. We'll deliver the safe and van to Gertrude's house and return here. I'll contact you when we've gotten the money out of the safe and then I'll arrange for the distribution of the money. You have to keep your mouths shut. No talking to anyone at the scene. I hope I've made it clear that you can't ever talk about this to anyone, including your mother and your slut. If I hear any loose talk, you'll be in serious trouble. Get your outfits on, get into the van and don't do anything stupid along the way to draw attention to yourself. Let's go!"

As the thugs got into the van, Randall observed that they actually looked like a trained military war party. What a day! He had trained his troops well. He could already taste the sweet elixir of success.

— 4 —

Thomas Reed got up early that same morning and marveled at the beautiful day that was developing. As fate would have it, or perhaps one could throw in a Greek god or two for the happenstance, Reed and Randall were both marveling at their good fortune to be alive on this glorious day. Randall, the quintessential sociopath and egomaniac, was always thrilled at the thought of delivering pain to another human. *Could there be any greater high than to experience the rush of power when delivering death to another human?*

On Reed's part, why should he not be happy? In spite of his checkered history in business and his run-in with the Department of Human Services over his activities as a foster parent, he was now a respected businessman in Fort Walton Beach. He and his wife, Delores, were well received in Fort Walton as a generous couple who devoted their lives to caring for disabled children. They had six such children living in this beautiful house, all of whom were disabled. They had adopted four of the children and two were there under the foster care program. He had established the Reed Children's Special Needs Trust to help care for the children. Thomas and Delores, being childless, no doubt at some level actually loved these kids.

As Reed, at the age of fifty-three, contemplated his good fortune in life, he could not resist the smirk that formed on his face. *Who knew how profitable it would be to appear as a do-gooder?* Most people were happy to have someone else care for these kinds of children. A donation to a trust was much easier to soothe one's need to do good than to actually care for a disabled child. *What was that old commercial? "Promise them anything, but give them Chanel No. 5"?* Reed was comforted as he welcomed the new day with the knowledge that he had learned to play the game well.

As a respected member of the community who knew how to play the role, no one really questioned his car business or his pawnshop business. He knew that he didn't look or talk like a thief or a person who would deal with the Mexican drug cartel. The community knew Reed as a man of charity. "Yes, God is good," he mumbled to himself.

After his usual morning activities, dropping in on the car lot and checking two of the pawnshops, Reed returned home to take a nap. He and Delores, age fifty-one, often took a short nap in the afternoon. It was a time of rest and entertainment for this couple, who, in spite of their weaknesses, cared for each other.

Reed felt safe in his house. He kept his money in a secure safe and he had an excellent commercial surveillance system. He lived in a nice neighborhood where crime was unknown. *Well,* he thought as he lay there, *my activities of crime don't count, of course.*

At that exact moment, Thomas Reed and Randall Moss came face to face. Randall pumped six shots into Reed and five shots into Delores, in the chest, face and head.

One of the children, who was at home, said he heard this man say, "You're gonna die, one, two, three." Reed charged Randall, but both he and Delores were shot on the spot.

Matt Moss walked into the hallway leading to Reed's bedroom just in time to see Randall shoot Reed. "Randall!" yelled the Sr. Moss. "What the hell are you doing? I thought this was going to be a clean in and out job—no gun play!"

"Hell, Pop, this bastard deserved to die. He's just one dirty crook in my book, taking money from the poor folks and abusing these disabled kids. Besides, Reed attacked me. What was I to do? I shot him, so I had to shoot Delores."

"Son, we're in a hell of a mess here. You know they'll burn your ass here in Florida for killing folks, even if they're low-down thieves," Sr. Moss hissed in a shaky voice.

"Look, Pop, we got the scene covered. Nobody can identify us. If everybody keeps their mouth shut, we'll be fine."

"Yeah, remind me of that when they strap your butt down for the fatal shot of drugs! You know they'll find out Reed lent you money for your martial arts studio, so you'll be on their list."

Despite the excitement, the ninja thugs got the safe in the truck and sped away to Gertrude's house where the safe was to be stored, confident in the belief that the security camera was disabled and there were no reliable witnesses to the crime.

Unknown to this band of redneck warriors, the maid who was supposed to disable the security camera had failed in her task. Except for the actual shots fired in the bedroom, the digital security camera captured everything, including the arrival of the group in the red van. With the van's license plate clearly visible, it wouldn't take long for the police to run the group to ground.

Perhaps it is true that in the moment before certain death, a man's life flashes before his eyes. His memory may even continue until the soul leaves the body. If Reed could talk to us from where he is, perhaps he could confirm this phenomenon. Chic had studied this particular folklore, but he concluded that Christ was right on this subject. The man in hell who wanted to return to warn his brothers was denied this right because his brothers who had not responded in life would not believe a dead man's warning. By the same token, if Reed could return, it's likely that no one would believe him either.

The instant Randall burst into Reed's bedroom, he locked eyes with the killer and knew there was no mercy there. What he did in those last moments came from that lizard part of the brain where the body reacts and the mind is totally somewhere else. What the body did in that last instant he knew not, but his whole life seemed instantly to flash in his mind before he entered the eternal unknown.

What he saw in that flash memory was a demon, devouring him along with his family and all he loved. The young boy of his youth, bright with hope and promise, quickly turned to darkness as the demon devoured his very soul. In that moment of horror, Thomas Reed realized he loved no one but himself. He was to enter judgment in the belly of the beast along with Delores, clothed only in his dreams of power, money and fame. So it is that man enters and leaves life the same way: naked.

Had Reed had time in that last flash of his life story, he surely would have chosen to relive that glorious night when he was finally recognized for his wonderful work with the children …

"Now, Thomas, let me get that bowtie straight," Delores had said as she fussed over Thomas's tie.

"Delores, you know I don't like these damn monkey suits," Thomas had said as he smiled at himself in the mirror. His pride at his manly appearance in the mirror began to grow as he realized that he had finally beaten the bastards. All those damn social workers who had given him fits over the years were left gawking at his new image as a philanthropist.

And where are my bastard business partners who tried to bring me down all my adult life? I've beaten them all. Even those bastard drug lords from Mexico have had to get out of my way. My boss, Victor, can handle those Mexican freaks. Hell, I'm the biggest cog in Victor's machine in the Panhandle. Victor can't get along without me to handle the money and drug operation. Man, if I could just tell everybody what all I control, even those do-gooders would be amazed at me.

And so it was that night of celebrations of Thomas Reed's wonderful work with the disadvantaged and mentally handicapped youth that a cloud of faux humility floated into his mind: *Alas, no one can truly know how really great I am, not even Delores.*

— 5 —

Reed's success in the Florida Panhandle had not gone unnoticed by the cesspool of drug dealers, including competing Mexican drug cartels. Reed was known as the right-hand man of Victor, who was an elusive crime boss in the Panhandle. Reed understood that his organization was connected to the Sinaloa cartel for drugs. His circle of protection came from that cartel and, to a lesser degree, from a few contract enforcers that Victor provided. Everybody knew that it was just a matter of time before the fight for drug territory between the Mexican gangs would find its way to America, the mother lode of drug addicts.

Like termites boring through wood, out of sight, out of mind, the Zeta cartel from the Gulf of Mexico began to covet the northern Gulf of Mexico. They figured they were closer to the area and would be able to push out the cartel from Mexico City.

The first thrust began with Rhohelia from Monterey. Reed was at his car lot, talking to his lawyer friend, Albert Barnes, about one of his side businesses that he and Victor had off line, so to speak. At least that was Albert's view of what it was. As they say, there is no honor among thieves and everybody needs a profit center on the side.

Rhohelia had done his homework and knew that Reed was Victor's contact man with the Sinaloa cartel. Rhohelia came into Reed's office at the car lot, dressed in the usual dark business suit, polished shoes and crisp white shirt, carrying a briefcase. In July in Fort Walton, this may have appeared unusual, but Reed knew this was obviously a visitor from Mexico. This type of guy gets the title around marinas as "the suit."

"The suit" came in and politely asked if he could speak with Reed about a matter of interest to him and Victor. Hearing Victor's name sent off warning bells in Reed's head, so he asked Albert to step outside for a few minutes and invited Rhohelia to take a seat. "Well, Rhohelia, what can I do for you"?

"Mr. Reed, I know you are a busy man as am I. I pride myself on being direct and to the point."

"Feel free," said Reed. "Just cut the crap and tell me what you're doing in my office. I don't like damn suits like you anyway. Spit it out!"

"I'm here on a friendly visit on behalf of my clients in Monterey. We've been keeping an eye on the Panhandle and know that you and your group are dealing with our competitors from Mexico City. On the other hand, we are your neighbors and we can reach out and touch you a lot faster than that crowd in Mexico City."

"Now hold on here, you little shit. I'm not going to get in the middle of some butt fuck between you and the Mexicans. We're perfectly happy with our present friends. They're perfectly capable of protecting their territory. You better get out of here right now before I make a call and you find your head in one place and your body in another."

"Mr. Reed, I was hoping we could have a friendly conversation about a business deal with us. Even if you only used us part of the time, we'd make it worth your while. It's good for your pocketbook and healthy to do this the friendly way. Victor wouldn't know the difference. We'd start with just a little piece of the business to show you we know what we're doing."

"This conversation is over. I'm not going to risk a certain death with my present friends just to please some asshole like you. I tell you what—I'll give you this break. I won't turn my people on you before tomorrow. Then I'm going to tell my people everything about you. If I were you, I wouldn't let the sun go down before my ass was back in Monterey. Maybe there you can keep your head."

"It's been nice knowing you, Mr. Reed. Here's my card with a phone number where I can be reached for the next twenty-four hours if you change your mind. If I were you, I wouldn't let the sun come up on my ass without calling me on that number. Adios, amigo."

Without further farewell, Rhohelia turned tail, got into a black Mercedes convertible and sped away. Reed took down the tag number and made a couple of notes on the car description. He knew this was no casual meeting.

Reed promptly called Victor with the full details. Victor put the phone on hold and then came back and told Reed he would be there shortly.

Victor pulled up to Reed's car lot in his gray Porsche and called to Reed, "Reed, come over here. I'm in a hurry."

"Well, I hope you're on Rhohelia's ass. Here's his card with the phone number. You have his description already, along with his tag number."

"I'll tell you this, Reed; his ass will be fish bait tonight. The boss wants you to know that you made the right decision. We're going to call in some troops and nip this thing in the bud. We can't have this wide-open war like is going on in Mexico. Keep your eyes open and call me if you see any suspicious activity."

Victor gunned his Porsche out of Reed's lot before he could say anything in reply, but Reed felt that this problem would be quickly taken care of. Reed knew he had been in fights before, but fighting the Mexican cartel was a death wish. He fought down that nagging feeling that if these guys were really serious, his world was in for a serious shock.

"Thomas," called Albert, "what the hell is going on there? You guys look like you've seen a ghost."

"Nothing but business, Albert. I thought you had left."

"Yeah, I went down to the bar and got a drink. Looks like you could use one about now."

Albert and Reed left the car lot and went to a bar down the street. They settled into their usual corner where they had a good view of some young girl's ass as she exhibited her body to the pleasure of the men while leaning over the pool table to make her shot. It became obvious to their delight that somehow she found it necessary to lean over the table on every shot.

"Man, I needed this drink." Reed sighed. "There's always someone trying to make trouble."

"Yeah, that's right," chimed in Albert. "If anybody ever figures out how we're doing our little business, we'd be in deep shit. Our plan is foolproof as long as everyone keeps their mouth shut. Actually, Thomas, you and I are the only ones who know the details of this plan. I don't think Victor knows all the details. He just provides the money for the operations."

"You know, Albert, it's a shame you can't tell everybody about this. All your lawyer friends think you're a dumb shit, but you've come up with a plan that's pure genius. Let's drink to your genius idea."

"Salute," said Albert. "It takes both of us, Thomas. You've got to get the people in here to sign the paperwork for the deed and mortgage and other paperwork that goes with the loan. They've got to be stupid enough to sign a false name with the fake ID. You provide the people and they don't ask any questions. Of course, it's clear these people don't know what they're signing."

"These people I use," said Thomas, "I can use over and over. They do whatever I tell them."

"What makes this work," said Albert, "is that the people who actually own the property will never know about this. When the title company checks the records, they won't find the mortgage or deed we do because they only check the correct chain of title. Our mortgage and deed will never show up because our people don't own the property and aren't in the chain of title. On the other hand, anyone checking our records will see a bona fide loan file with a mortgage and deed for the most part. Since the outfit we sell the mortgage to is controlled by Victor, who provides us the money, this will pass as a clean washing of the money. When you analyze this, Thomas, our primary weakness lies with the people who sign our documents. They must be ignorant and silent about this operation. I just want to emphasize your importance to the security of our little operation."

Reed patted Albert on the back and said, "This is a smooth scheme. I bring you the money in cash in small amounts, which you deposit in your trust account. When we get up to a hundred thousand dollars or so, we close a loan in your office and get a check from your trust account in exchange for the signed deed on a piece of property we don't own. Victor gives me and you some cash on the side and everybody leaves happy. Nobody's hurt, certainly not the real property owners. As long as I keep my people quiet, we should be safe."

Albert, thinking about his cool money-washing scheme, knew that the scheme's complexity was beyond most of the local lawyers around this area. He knew the other lawyers thought he was a dumb bastard. He stammered and generally looked uncomfortable as a speaker. He knew he was a poor trial lawyer. Other lawyers looked upon him as an inferior lawyer as well as an inferior human being. Albert took a sip of his Amstel light, washed his negative mind of its impurities and refreshed his attitude with the thought of his girlfriend, Marie, whom he planned to see shortly. A little sport sex and a line of coke would take care of any problems he had right now.

Albert couldn't help but think that if his lawyer buddies knew about his brilliant scheme, they would appreciate his keen legal mind. They would never know how smart he really was. *Well, I'm making more money than any of them, so they can just eat shit*, he thought to himself.

"What's up, Albert?" said Thomas. "Looks like you're floating on some cloud nine over there. That girl's ass is nice, but not that nice."

"You might be surprised," Albert said. "I hear she's got some real space pussy."

"Yeah, what's that supposed to mean?"

"That means that every time you get a piece of ass, you blow out some brain matter when you shoot your wad."

"Hell, Albert, when you get my age, such thinking is history. You only think about how youth is wasted on the young."

Albert and Thomas would have been surprised to know that Victor's people were all aware of this business. They knew it was not really off line and let them continue in their ignorance as a form of firewall.

As Albert and Thomas covered their worries with drink, Rhohelia was cruising down Highway 98, thinking about his conversation with his superior in Monterey. His report was not good and the boys in Monterey were unhappy. As Rhohelia approached the traffic light at the intersection of Highway 298 near Haven Park, he observed a car off the road across the street, but before he could react to what he saw, the small-bore .22 caliber hollow-point bullet struck him in the left eye. There was no noise from the silenced weapon and no one noticed anything was wrong until Rhohelia's car horn began to blow. Someone in line behind him finally got out of their car, went to Rhohelia's car and saw that the driver had collapsed over the passenger seat. The entry wound was so small and there was no exit wound, so it took a second to realize the driver was dead. By this time, the other car was gone and there were virtually no witnesses to the murder in broad daylight.

Because Rhohelia had a fake driver's license, a stolen vehicle and carried nothing on him that properly identified him, the police had a John Doe murder. There was certainly nothing to indicate that this death marked the first volley in the Mexican battle over which of the cartels would control Florida's Panhandle.

Victor got the call from the assassin as they pulled into the parking lot of the pub where Reed and Albert Barnes were drowning their perceived problems. "Victor," said the first assassin, "we collected the rent."

"Good, good," said Victor. "Now go in the pub and have a drink. Keep an eye on Reed and Barnes. Make sure they don't have any other bill collectors coming by. I don't think I have to remind you to blend in. I don't want Thomas to know we have him under protection or surveillance."

The first assassin grunted and disconnected. Then he sent in his partner, who was a smaller guy and unknown to both Thomas Reed and Albert Barnes.

— 6 —

Monterey, Mexico, is a lovely industrial town in northeastern Mexico, just a comfortable drive from Laredo, Texas, down Mexico Highway 85. Mexican drug cartels, however, have spoiled what would otherwise be a great place to live.

The kingpins of the Zeta cartel met at the palatial home of "Hernandez" the day after Rhohelia was assassinated in Pensacola. The mysterious murder made the news. It didn't take long for them to understand that Thomas or someone in his operation assassinated Rhohelia.

Hernandez lived in a twelve thousand square feet mansion constructed in the Spaniard style of red tile roof and white stucco, with marble and tile throughout the inside. It was perched in the mountains west of Monterey, surrounded by a five thousand acre cattle ranch. A beautiful fortress by any measure.

Hernandez, Jorge and Peppi controlled the Zeta cartel. Hernandez was the head boss assisted by Jorge and Peppi. Jorge was the head enforcer and Peppi was in control of the money. Jorge and Peppi flew in earlier that same day in their separate private jets to the private airport on Hernandez's ranch.

The night air was cool, so the men sat around the open fire pit where a half steer was on a spit cooking as they drank Louis XIII de Re'my Martin cognac and smoked Cuban cigars. It took thirty minutes for the cognac to warm the men to the problems at hand.

Jorge was, as usual, the first to speak up. He was the firebrand and cold-blooded killer in the group. Jorge delighted in chopping off heads himself, which he considered a perk of his job. He never understood why some of these guys like to delegate this particular pleasure. "Look here," said Jorge," if we expect to take this territory from Sinaloa, we've got to be willing to fight it out. We have a tactical advantage over the Sinaloa because our people are physically closer to the northern Gulf. I know we do some business in that area, but we don't control it."

Hernandez then spoke up. "We all know that if we go in and try to control this area, we're going to have a bloody war. Is that what we want? We still make plenty of money in that area without trying to control the entire retail end of the business. Even Sinaloa can't stop us from selling to our dealers. What we don't want is open war in Pensacola between the Sinaloa and Zetas. If we have heads rolling in the streets of Pensacola, we're asking for big trouble."

"What do you suggest?" asked Peppi.

"First," said Hernandez, "we need to take out Reed. We can follow the method used by Reed's operation in killing Rhohelia. Let's hire it out to some local thug. They can kill Reed without it looking like a drug deal gone bad. Victor, of course, will get the message. The Sinaloa cartel will get the information and they'll know that we're asserting ourselves. We'll take out Reed and see what happens. What we shouldn't do is jeopardize our contact with dealers by encouraging the Sinaloa to declare all-out war with the Zetas. You know guys, the ATF got things so confused and screwed up with their fast and furious operation that nobody will know what's going on for certain. This will give us cover while we decide how far to push this affair."

After some discussion, including thinking about their own mortality in case of an all-out war, which would bring the US authorities down on them all, the group agreed to seek out Randall Moss, an egotistical hood in Fort Walton that no one would associate with them.

"Jorge," said Hernandez, "get one of our dealers out of Texas to go hire Randall Moss. Tell him anything you like, but there is to be no trace back to us. Got it?"

"Yes, sir," said Jorge. "I'd sort of like to whack him myself, but I'll get somebody else to do the job."

Hernandez correctly guessed that if Randall talked, nobody would believe his story about being a hired assassin. It was common knowledge among the initiated that Randall Moss boasted about being a hired killer often without anything to back it up. He was the quintessential blow hard. His own mother wouldn't believe him on a stack of Bibles. Everyone, however, would believe that he killed Reed as part of a robbery. It was going to be the job of the agent who hired Randall to make certain that this looked like a robbery gone bad and not an assassination. Hernandez calculated the dumb shit would like the idea. He would get extra money in the robbery and probably would think the whole thing was his idea.

From Hernandez's point of view, a perfect crime. It would be revenge without alarming the US authorities or the Sinaloa.

"Well, I think we've spent enough time on business," announced Hernandez. The servants came with the choice parts of the grilled beef and served the men while a lovely young lady dressed in a French waitress outfit served more cognac. As the night wore on, the men disappeared to their private rooms with their own lovely lady for dessert.

Perhaps in that last moment for Thomas Reed, that feeling of doom he had so carefully suppressed was released, for surely he knew the minute he was contacted by Rhohelia his life was over. Surely Rhohelia knew when he was rebuffed by Reed that his life was over.

Later, on the same night as Reed's robbery and murder, a hasty meeting was called by Victor Gomez, the right-hand man of Boss, a well-known businessman in Pensacola, Florida. The physical beauty of Boss's office, which was located on Pensacola Bay, adjacent to the marina where Boss kept his sixty-five-foot cruising yacht, was anything but peaceful this lovely night.

"Boss, I hated to interrupt your dinner, but we have a problem. Thomas and Delores Reed were murdered this afternoon and the safe was taken from his house."

"We can't have that, Victor. There are too many documents in his files that could be used to trace his operations back to us."

"I never did feel safe using that bastard as a vehicle to help launder some of our assets. I never trusted him," Victor said.

"It's the risk of doing business. Everything you do leaves some kind of trail, especially handling money. There's no way to do business in a vacuum. That's the reason I've got you. Your job is to keep the low-lifers in line and provide cover for me," retorted Boss.

"I understand, Boss. My sources have informed me that they believe the Mexican mafia took a contract out on Reed. I don't know, but this could be related to that visit to Reed by Rhohelia last month. I'd guess it might be pay back for us killing their man."

"Could be, Victor. Our Mexicans don't think they're being challenged yet. Do we have anything specific about who was involved in the murder?"

"Boss, we got a little information from one of our dealers who claims he was at a bar a couple of nights ago and overheard this little queer bragging to his buddy about being in a ninja gang which was going to rob some guy named Thomas. The kid was pretty drunk and my dealer thought he was just shooting some shit to his stud. You know how kids are.

"I checked up on the kid and found out he is good friends with Randall Moss. I remember Moss. He used to work with Reed. This kid also mentioned the name of Gertrude, who he claims was in charge of plans for the robbery. Moss has been known to run around with a Gertrude and by reputation she would be the one to take charge. Moss wouldn't have enough brains to plan this killing and dispose of the safe and the money."

"I suspect Gertrude has the safe. I've already sent some of the boys to check out a few things, especially Gertrude's house and see what we can find."

"We have to get that safe back fast," said Boss. "We can't let the police or Moss and his crew get into it. Find it and get it back immediately. Use as few guys as necessary. We don't need to have any loose lips to add to the problem."

"You got it, Boss. I'll let you know as soon as I have a line on the safe."

"Don't delay, Victor. As soon as you have a make on where the safe is, move in and take it. If you're discovered, you know what to do, but it's far better if get out of there with the safe without encounter and without gunplay."

When Victor left, Boss took the opportunity to rare back in his big chair at his office, place his feet on the deck railing and enjoy the full moon reflecting on Pensacola Bay. *How great it would be*, he thought, *if you could simply rely on people to do their job. Just take care of business, that's all.* In the honest side of his operations, as well as the money laundering and drug part of his operations, the limits were set by the workers, who for the most part were dedicated to their own selfish goals, not the business. *What do I expect?* thought Boss. *It's the nature of man to steal. Well, that was the reason he made the big bucks. You can't trust people and you have to handle the cash transactions yourself.* Using Victor or a go between in some of the transactions gave him a level of protection, but the weakness was that someone else knew enough about his business to cause concern. *If we get those records in Reed's safe before the police do, then I'm still safe and hidden from prying eyes*, reasoned Boss.

Boss's immediate concern was whether to notify his handlers in Boston of the problem. While he had a high degree of independence, Boston was clearly in charge. The flow of all money was at their command. All the offshore banking and the wiring of money to local banks to fund loans was under their strict control. All payments on mortgage and receipts from legal enterprises were in their control. All the various religious and charitable corporations used as channels for money flow were designed and manipulated by Boston. The whole organization was a quintessential daisy chain for drug money flowing out of Mexico to fund much of the operations that were handled between Boston and Mexico.

Boss was the front man in the southeast and actually operated the legitimate businesses. His was the duty to handle the flow of cash from drugs and shady enterprises into legitimate enterprises. The flow of cash was his biggest responsibility. Maintaining a clean image was his biggest challenge. It was in the handling of cash and designing the daisy chain of corporations where Boss had the confidence of his mentors. Boss was in charge of the southeast, although he was primarily responsible for the interrelationship of all the corporations in the chain. There were several other operatives like him, although he didn't personally know how many. Boss was certain that none of the other operators could identify any of the other operators.

Replacing Reed would be a problem. It would be up to Boston to replace Reed or at least to approve his replacement. Boss closed his eyes and allowed the situation to rattle around in his mind until he felt the solution form. Boss trusted his instincts and his instincts told him he was safe for the time being. Once he got the safe back, he would carefully go through all the records and make sure his tracks were covered. Only essential information would be retained in a safe place. Records from most of the business would have to be purged. *Well*, he thought, *this is a good time to update record keeping and carefully destroy the old records.*

Satisfied that he could safely contain his operation, he decided to get his superiors in Boston on the line.

Boss got out his special encrypted phone and placed a call to Boston to speak to his contact, identified only as Number One. "Number One," said Boss, "I need to bring you up to date on my activities for the last quarter."

"Go ahead." Boss proceeded to give a full operations' report, giving the bottom line on income, expenses and profits. Boss kept a running activity report on the transfer of cash between the banks and the cash flow from the various daisy chain corporations. Boss then gave a full report on the Reed murder and his request for a replacement.

"We'll have a man down there within the next two weeks," Number One said. "We've got a guy in New Mexico that can handle Thomas Reed's business. He's actually trained in our full operation. You need to keep us posted on this problem. If they get too close, we may have to move you to another area. We can't have the authorities digging into our money operations or any connection that would lead to our legitimate enterprises. I don't have to remind you that once we've approved the data and created our archive, you must destroy all of your local records. We must limit how far the government can go back into our operations."

Boss knew this was no friendly chat; it was a clear threat. There were *no second chances in this operation and retirement was … well, why think about that.*

Boss had little faith in being transferred to another location, so he understood this message to be *succeed—or else.* "Okay," said Boss, with a false bravado born of arrogance, "we've got things under control here. I'll have that safe secured within twenty-four hours."

"Don't fail," was the simple reply from Number One, followed by an abrupt disconnecting of the call.

Boss, knowing the seriousness of his position, stood and retreated to his yacht, which represented to him his cave. In this closed, encapsulated space, his spirit returned to the womb and his soul yearned for spiritual cleansing. Boss lay on his bunk in the dark and allowed his mind to drift. The gentle rocking of the boat and the closed space soothed the lizard part of his brain into the illusion of safety from all harm. When Boss awoke with the rising sun the next morning, it was with a renewed spirit of elation, ready to attack his fate. When he's lived this kind of life, a man knows that remorse over his past offenses can't be part of his conscious thought.

— 7 —

The sun was dipping below the horizon in Pensacola Bay when Victor got word from his sources that the safe was located at Gertrude's house in Fort Walton, along with her red van, which was used in the robbery-murder. Chatter on the police radio and loose talk from the police department revealed that the surveillance camera at Reed's house had pretty much captured the entire scene in living color. While the police, at this point, had not identified the suspects, it was obvious that the merry band of ninja robbers would quickly be apprehended.

Victor got to work immediately. He called Boss to give him the news and decided to go after the safe without delay. They didn't have time to be cute. A frontal attack was called for and any interference would be eliminated with lethal force.

Victor got his buddies, Sam and Fred, to handle the caper. They secured a dolly and other equipment and took off to Gertrude's house. By the time they got there, it was dark. A yellowish full moon provided the proper backlight for what was about to happen.

Victor had given them the plan of attack. He had already obtained information on the floor plan of Gertrude's house from a friend who worked in the Fort Walton Beach Building Inspector's office. They believed that the safe was still in the red van, which was in the carport with the door down and locked. There was no quick way to recover the safe other than a home invasion.

"Fred," explained Sam, "we're going in the back door. Eliminate Gertrude and any witnesses that may be there. I'll then drive the truck to the back of the house. You open the carport door and we'll load the safe onto the truck and get out of there. You get the door open and be ready to do what I tell you. Keep your gloves on and be sure to put on those shoe covers. We don't want to leave any traceable evidence around."

Sam drove by Gertrude's house and saw that it was fairly isolated on its wooded lot. There were houses in the general neighborhood, but no one had a clear view of Gertrude's house. He observed that the driveway was paved leading to the carport, which was in the back of the house. There was no traffic on the road at the time. He guessed everyone was busy with dinner, which was good. Two streetlights and the light in the back yard needed to be dealt with.

"Fred, get the pellet gun from the back seat. I'm going to slow down and you take out those lights."

"Why can't I use my .22 caliber? It would be a lot easier to shoot out the light with the .22."

"Don't be a smart ass, Fred. You're no damn comedian. You know a .22 would make too much noise. Use that air gun like I told you. Nobody can hear that."

After five shots, Fred finally shot out the three lights. The street was now dark.

Sam came to a stop along the curb where they took a few minutes to study the house. They could see two cars in the back yard and there were some lights on in the house. Although they could see no activity, they were sure that Gertrude had company this night. The wet work was going to get wetter.

Sam cut off the lights and quietly pulled into the driveway, which led around the house to the enclosed carport. Sam was careful to stay on the paved area so as not to leave any tire marks. "Okay, Fred, you got your instructions. Let's go."

As Sam and Fred prepared to break into Gertrude's house, the pressing of human flesh that was taking place inside would have pleased any sex therapist. Gertrude had one of her sex slaves, Jim, over for a little group session of free love. Lights were low, but the activity was hot. Gertrude and Jim had a little head start on Suzy, who had arrived a little late.

"Gertrude," said Suzy, "keep warming Jim up while I take a quick shower." Gertrude hardly needed any direction in this area from Suzy. She and Jim were already nude and Gertrude was kissing Jim in all the right places.

The bathroom was off the bedroom and was quite a fancy affair. There was an inside and outside shower. The outside shower was enclosed but was open at the top so you could look at the sky while you showered. There was a small Japanese garden within the walled shower, along with a seating area, which was a favorite place of Gertrude's sex partners.

Suzy observed the festivities as she entered the shower and was a little perturbed that Gertrude was ahead of her, so she called out for Gertrude to go slow until she got there. "You bet," Gertrude replied.

Suzy decided to use the outside shower to gain the romantic ambiance provided by the full harvest moon while washing her naked body of the day's activities. The thought of the threesome with Jim and Gertrude had her juices flowing.

As Suzy shut the shower door and started the shower, Sam and Fred entered the house. Fortunately, for Suzy, the shower door was shut, so Sam didn't see her as he came into the bedroom. Sam came through the door and without hesitation shot both Gertrude and Jim in the head. Not more than a minute had elapsed from the time they came into the house until Gertrude and Jim lay dead in the bed, Gertrude atop Jim.

Sam yelled to Fred to open the garage door and get the dolly while he looked around. Sam used a 7mm pistol in this operation, loaded with hollow-point bullets. There was not enough noise to carry outside the house.

As Sam made sure the couple on the bed was dead, he heard the faint sound of water running in the shower. He quickly ran to the bathroom but found it empty. He went to the outside shower and there was no one there. He cut off the water and looked around, as it seemed obvious that somebody had been there when he entered the house. The couple, now dead in the bed, were in the act of fornication when he shot them, so someone else had to be in the shower. *What had they seen or heard?* He saw that the bench located in the outside shower was placed against the wall. He gathered that someone agile and athletic might be able to mount the wall and escape to the outside. He made one attempt but was unable to mount the wall.

Sam then yelled to Fred to look outside for whoever had been in the house. He ran from the bathroom and as he made the turn out of the bed-room, he heard the squealing tires of an escaping car. Sam and Fred got outside just in time to see the car speeding off down the dark street. "Can you identify the car, Fred?"

"Not really. It looked like a white convertible, but I can't be sure about the model and I couldn't see the driver."

"Shit. We don't have time to chase the car. Whoever it was can't identify us, but we've got to move fast before they call the police." It took less than ten minutes for them to load the safe in their truck and pull onto the dark roadway.

Suzy had just stepped into the shower when she heard the shots. Her innate sense of self-preservation immediately took over. She slid the bench against the outside wall, jumped onto the bench, bounced up to catch the top of the wall and then smoothly propelled herself over the wall and onto the ground. Naked as the day of her birth, she darted to her car, jumped in and as fortune would have it, she had left her purse with the keys in it, on the floor under the front seat, a bad habit she had developed. An eternity seemed to pass as she fumbled through her purse for the keys. She finally found them and was able to get away before they could stop her. "Thank God!" To her knowledge, she had left no identification around Gertrude's house; her clothes were in the bathroom, but there was nothing there to identify her. As she sped away she saw the two men come out of the house looking in her direction. She didn't believe they could actually identify her.

Would they come after her? Should she call the police? Now, or after she got some clothes on? What in the hell had Gertrude done? She had not slowed enough to see whether Gertrude and Jim were dead or exactly what had taken place. Maybe she just panicked and Gertrude was okay. *If I call 911,* she thought, *I would be identified. Do I want to be identified?* As confused as she was, Suzy had enough presence of mind to follow a winding route to make sure no one was following her. Besides, driving her white BMW convertible naked required her to keep to the dark streets. She made it home in one piece.

After much soul searching, Suzy called 911. From that moment on, she knew her life would never be the same. She knew her secret sex life would now become part of the public domain. Her second thought was Chic Sparks. She didn't know him well, but she knew his reputation. In her gut, she knew that he could help her— but —*would he? Why would he?*

— 8 —

When in town, Chic always met on Sunday nights with the Fish House Gang to play penny poker at Ken Renfro's house. Ken had a boathouse behind his home on a small slough off Choctawhatchee Bay. The boathouse was a two-story affair with a nice meeting room on the second floor. Ken had his 2009 Donzi 382R, a fast-performing cigarette boat, hoisted so that he could walk out of the second-floor game room, step into the Donzi racer, lower himself into the water and be in Destin, Florida, within fifteen minutes. If there was a better place to play penny poker or a better group to play poker with, Chic could not find them.

Take Ken. What a great guy! Ken was a native of Tennessee, but he had been in the mortgage business in Pensacola for the last fifteen years. He graduated from Vanderbilt and gained a reputation in the area as an outstanding business leader. Judging by his man toys and the ten-thousand-square-foot house on Choctawhatchee Bay, there was no cash flow problem. Ken was still a fit two hundred pounds at six feet and looked like he could still play fullback as he did at Vanderbilt.

Ken's mortgage company specialized in commercial loans, although occasionally they dabbled in the residential market. He also operated a company that developed, operated and managed commercial properties for him as well as for third parties. The Fish House Gang knew he had some interest in a commercial fishing boat and a fifty-foot sailboat with crew located in Destin Harbor, Florida, by the name of *Amadee*. With his new 500SL Mercedes, Ken cut quite a figure around town and was considered the most eligible bachelor in the Panhandle area, even though he was no spring chicken at age forty-two. Somehow, Ken was able to appear unimpressed with his wealth while radiating gravitas with his toys.

No card game would be complete without Ken and his tall tales of adventure. In truth, everyone at the table secretly envied Ken's good looks, his bevy of fast women, his physical power, his man toys and money.

Ken always teased Chic about wearing lace underwear while on a singing gig. All the gang joined in, but Ken was the leader. Chic had enough self-assurance to join in the fun. Everyone knew, however, that Chic was the last guy in the world you would challenge to a fight. At six feet two inches and 215 pounds of muscle and holding a black belt in Karate, even Ken would hide behind Chic in a bar fight.

At cards, Chic was top dog. He was fairly good at card counting, but his gift was reading an opponent's mind, which was plain magic. When he fixed on you with his piercing green eyes, it seemed like the devil himself had taken possession of your mind. It was disarming to play poker with a guy that seemed to possess the power to strip your soul bare with a stare. Chic knew full well that he had this ability and he used it with great aplomb in cards as well as in his profession. Chic wouldn't admit it, but he knew he had an effect on the young ladies, even though he avoided the entrapment of matrimony. Chic was at that age when he was questioning whether or not it had been good to avoid settling down to a solid domestic life with a good woman.

Chic was the rudder of the Fish House Gang. With his good nature, wit and natural leadership ability, he was able to smooth out the rough places and keep the game on a light tone.

As with any group like this, there were plenty of characters to keep things interesting and sometimes even informative. Solving local crimes was always the prime topic of conversation.

Take Sydney Mullis, otherwise known as the "Judge," except at the card game, where he was called "Syd." Syd was the senior judge in Escambia County, Florida, where Pensacola is located. At age sixty-eight, Syd was not exactly of the modern world. At five feet ten inches and 250 pounds, Syd was a blast from the past. He had a big voice, heavy eyebrows, a permanent scowl on his face and the general demeanor of an executioner. He was able to put the fear of God in every lawyer in his courtroom. At the card games, however, Syd's growl was like a friendly roar of a docile lion.

Syd had two bad habits. One was his tendency to write bad checks. This was not a problem because everyone knew to call old Ralph Cox and he would take care of the bad checks. The other bad habit was women. All lawyers knew if they represented the husband in a divorce case with a good-looking woman on the other side, they were in trouble. Syd was known to involve himself with several ladies who came before his court for one reason or another. No one had the guts to challenge Syd on his womanizing.

Aside from Syd's human flaws, his bark and arrogant behavior, he was an outstanding jurist and a hell of a poker player. His dry wit and lawyer jokes were necessary adjuncts to the overall personality of the Fish House Gang.

Percy Greene was the only black member of the Fish House Gang. Percy was a gentleman and a scholar. He was a graduate from the horticulture school at Tuskegee Institute in Alabama. Percy had a successful landscaping business in the area. Although Percy did not have to be hands on, he still put in a full day of hard labor. This was the reason Percy could maintain a slim 155 pounds on his six-foot frame. Percy was a jolly guy with a sharp wit and liked to discuss politics, religion and philosophy. At times, Percy and Chic entertained the group with their deep discussions about religion. There was that time when Percy almost convinced Chic that Jesus was a black man. No one could tell if these guys were serious or just tongue in cheek. Percy managed to hide his hand with a good poker face and his constant needling of the Fish House Gang worked as an effective diversion.

Bob Funk, at thirty-five, was the youngest player in the Fish House Gang. He had a large crop of prematurely gray hair, which helped his stage presence with jurors and women. He had a solo law practice in Destin, Florida. Bob had a low Southern drawl and usually had a serious expression on his face. The way Bob dressed and his general demeanor qualified Bob as one the "good old boys".

Bob came from a military family that often moved. His father was a first sergeant in the army who was prone to beat up the entire family when he got drunk. Bob wore the emotional scars of his childhood. Bob was a friendly guy with unlimited talent to influence people, but floating around him was an aurora of tragedy. His great talent was weighed down by heavy drinking, smoking, wild women and, some believed, drugs. Bob was the life of every party, drunk or sober. He had a quick wit and the ability to spin a tall tale that captivated the entire gang. The Fish House Gang could not exist without this live wire.

Bob always controlled his drinking at the Fish House Gang's card parties, but not in Las Vegas. Drinking, snorting and flirting with the girls at the gambling table was a recipe for disaster. He was bailed out of Las Vegas several times by Ken Renfro, a regular client. The general wisdom was that Bob, to pay his gambling debts, was under the complete control of Ken. But with Bob, who cared about those little problems when a good time was had by all?

Ralph Cox was an old real estate man from the old school. Ralph was a special friend of Judge Mullis—the go-to man who covered the Judge's bad checks.

Ralph looked like an old country squire. At five feet eight inches, a rotund 190 pounds and with gray hair, he looked and felt like your favorite uncle. Ralph tried to complete a real estate deal of some kind, big or small, every day. This attitude made Ralph a rich man. His primary real estate interest was low-class rental property, primarily in the black community. His familiarity with the black community educated him in the fine art of voodoo. Ralph was a master. He could cast a spell with the best of the witch doctors. When he went through one of his rental houses, he always scattered about what he called grave dust. He had that little sparkle in his eyes like the cat that just swallowed the canary. His favorite game was to convince some uneducated group of blacks that he was once a black man. He would then disclose how he became a white man.

Ralph was as astute at poker as he was at real estate. He would take your money with eyes sparkling and a gravelly chuckle. Made you feel like your favorite uncle had just picked your pocket. Basically, Ralph tried his voodoo on the members of the gang. Not a bad tactic in a card game.

The poker game began at six on Sunday afternoon in the two-story boathouse at Ken's place. Ken had arranged for the cook and one server to keep the food and drinks flowing. Emma was a hell of a cook and tonight was the usual fair: fresh catfish, hush puppies, french fries, pickles and onions. For dessert, Emma had prepared her specialty, buttermilk pie. For appetizers, the boys had some wonderful Apalachicola oysters.

"Hey, Syd," said Bob, "how many oysters have you had? You need to save some for the rest of us."

"Now, Bob, you know I'm the Judge and I'm entitled to all the damn oysters my fat ass can handle."

"At this rate," Bob said with the usual smirk on his face, "I'm going to have to go back down to Joe Patti's and get some more oysters."

"Hell, Bob, tell that old Greek to give me some good ones this time."

Ralph joined in with his usual emphasis on Emma's pie. "You boys can have all those snotty oysters; just make sure you save me a big slice of Emma's pie."

After stuffing their faces, the boys took their places at the poker table.

Faye, the girl in charge of drinks, was wearing a short little dress, which displayed her long legs and other vital parts of her anatomy. She sternly admonished Syd: "Keep your hands off my ass, Syd. Where do you think you are, in court?"

"Now, be nice to an old man, Faye. You know I can't do anything but look and you sure got a nice ass to look at."

"Okay, Syd, you look, but keep your hands in your pockets," said Faye as she walked off half-smirking and half-pissed.

"Yes, ma'am." Syd gave a look like some hurt dog sulking in the corner.

"Okay," said Chic, "let's get this game underway. Whose deal is it?"

"Mine," said Ken. "Ante up."

The game finally settled into its usual pattern, with the guys pulling each other's chains and, if possible, trying to divert their attention from the game.

"Have you boys ever thought about how much brain power we expend on this silly-ass game of penny ante poker?" Bob asked. "If we were playing for some real money, it would be different, but we take this game as seriously as if we had something at stake. All we get out of this game is a full belly and a frustrated libido."

"You're right about that," replied Ralph, "but you remember why we want to play penny ante poker, don't you?"

"You talking about that robbery a few years ago?" asked Bob. "I guess we did have a good reason to go to penny ante poker. There's always some crook willing to spoil a good thing. Did they ever find those two guys?"

Chic, being familiar with the case, reminded them that they got some DNA from the door facing where one of the robbers had injured himself, but the police could not find a match.

"Speaking of crooks in this town," said Ralph, "how about those murders last week of Thomas Reed and his wife and then the double murder of Gertrude and her boyfriend? This damn place is suddenly eaten up with murders. What the hell's going on? What do you think, Syd?"

"Well, Ralph, I don't really know more than what's in the paper. It looks like that bunch that killed Reed was pretty stupid. The whole thing was recorded on video and all the crooks are in custody. When you get a crowd like that, they all sing like canaries. Now, this Gertrude girl … seems she was involved in the robbery somehow, but it's hard to say why she and her boyfriend were killed. I understand the boyfriend was married, but the wife has an alibi and this was obviously a professional hit."

Syd continued, "The connection may be the safe, since that was the object of the robbery and the crooks claim that the safe was delivered to Gertrude's house. The safe has not been recovered, so there's a high probability that Gertrude's murder is related to the disappearance of the safe. This is troubling because it means that there was a much bigger group than the ninjas involved in this, because it's accepted that the ninjas did not kill Gertrude."

"That's a hell of a supposition there, Syd," said Ken. "Must have been a lot of money in that safe to get that many people involved and somehow cause four murders. Do you think all these people were working for the same outfit?"

"Hard to say," said Chic. "I think we can assume that there was a relationship between Reed and the ninjas. Somebody in that group knew enough about Reed's home and habits to pull off the robbery. There's also a rumor that Randall was hired for the killing, although it may be just bragging on his part. It is possible that the ninjas and the group that killed Gertrude could be connected, but I don't think they are. At this point, the prosecutors have a strong case against the ninjas in Reed's death and they can get a conviction without trying to tie the two incidents together. In fact, it would complicate the Reed murder trial by tying them to Gertrude's murder."

"What you're saying then," said Ralph, "is that it's not worth the DA's time to tie the two together since it's clear that the ninjas were not directly involved with Gertrude's murder."

"That's right," said Chic. "The missing link is the safe. The ninjas took the safe and the second group stole the safe. Apparently, four murders have been committed over this safe, which is now missing. Whether the murders are somehow related, there is a general agreement that the contents of the safe would tie these murders together. It seems like Randall, on the way to a simple murder, ran into a bunch of killer bees."

Ken and Bob groaned a little at all this intrigue and Bob remarked, "Chic, damned if you don't sound like Sherlock Holmes!"

"Yeah," said Ken, "let's get this game underway."

"Y'all are right. We'll never solve these murders anyway. Probably some drugs involved, as there always is these days when you see multiple murders. I'll match your five cents and raise you ten cents," said Chic.

"You going to need to borrow some money to cover yourself?" asked Percy.

"No, but I'm glad you're covering my rear."

— 9 —

Later that same night, Boss sat in his shorts on his patio, looking out to sea at a full moon, smoking his Cuban cigar.

He was satisfied in the belief that the boys in Boston trusted him and had made it possible to operate without the appearance of outside control. Boston sent a tough guy to replace Reed, named George Currier. Boss knew you had to be tough to survive in the drug world of New Mexico.

As he sat there, a cloud covered the moon; a cool breeze began to blow. Through the palms, the sound of a dog barking in the distance evoked a feeling of dread. Boss suddenly felt an evil veil engulf his mind. He shook himself awake in order to escape the evil spirit that had invaded his peaceful reverie. Boss recognized this veil of doubt that captured his mind when he floated between sleep and awakening. Yes, his business was dangerous, but he couldn't dwell on the dangers of falling off the tightrope he walked every day. Boss retreated to his lair, deep in the boat, where he sought peace in a closed space, rocked by Neptune's rhythmic tide. It was there that his psyche returned to his mother's womb.

— 10 —

Monday morning following the rousing poker game, Chic met with Detective Heath Moore of the Fort Walton Police Department at Joe & Eddie's, one of their breakfast places, to discuss his thoughts on the recent murders.

"Chic, I'm sure you've kept up with the recent murders in the area. We've got the murder of Reed and his wife, the murder of Gertrude and her lover, the disappearance of the safe and the murder of a John Doe. The DA is not interested in spending a lot of time on trying to tie all this together. The DA has Randall Moss by the neck. With the high-resolution color video of the Reed murders and the loose lips of the coconspirators, the whole crowd is likely to get the death penalty.

"Based on what has been said by the group of ninjas, they have no idea who stole the safe from Gertrude. Randall wants us to believe he was hired to kill Reed, but nobody believes anyone would be stupid enough to hire Randall for anything, much less a murder. He has been spending some money lately, but there's no evidence he was doing anything but robbing Thomas Reed and that he got a little carried away with himself.

"The mystery is how another group found out about the robbery so fast and was able to locate and grab the safe as fast as they did. Then this John Doe murder has the earmark of a gang murder. What do you think, Chic?"

"I know there is the underlying issue of how much time and money the city is willing to spend on a thorough investigation to explore how these crimes are related, if at all. I assume that the reason you're asking me to come up with some ideas is because I'm cheap."

"You're right in that regard," Heath said. "It's cheaper for us to let you help us narrow down our search. After all, trying to see if there's some connection may just be a witch hunt."

"Well, since this is official business, Heath, I hope you're going to be paying for breakfast today."

"I guess I can spring for that as long as you order the special for five bucks," said Heath. We can't pay for that omelet you usually get."

"Can you pay for my orange juice?"

"If you stick to the small glass, I guess we can cover it."

"Heath, tell the Chief I'm cheap, but not that cheap."

"Ah, order what you want, Chic. What's life worth if I can't pull your chain?"

"Here comes the waitress, Heath. Let's give her our order and then I'll be ready to dig into the case."

When the waitress left, Chic stared into the detective's eyes and embarked on his first shot at the facts. "There has to be drugs involved at the bottom of this. The fight over the safe tells me that there may be money there, but the keen interest has to be directed toward the information contained in the safe. If that were the case, I would assume that the Reed murder was about the money. Gertrude's murder was about the information. You can't just assume, however, that the two murders are related. The connection is the information. What would Reed have in his safe that would instigate the second murder? Actually, what person or group would Reed have close enough contact with to be in possession of their sensitive documents?"

"As you know," Heath said, "Reed has a checkered past in business deal- ing and with the Department of Human Resources. I would describe him as a petty thief and a loan shark. Somehow, he's been able to polish the souse's ear into a silk purse and sell himself as a good guy. I find it amazing that he died as a well-respected citizen. His car business seems to be doing well and he has some contact with several pawnshops. So he went from being a low-class loan shark and petty thief to the big time. The question is how did he do this so quickly? Occasionally we get rumors of drug dealings, which are common around car lots, but no solid complaints. The John Doe killing looks like a drug hit, but that's a guess and we can't connect that killing to Reed. Still, that's a lot of killing going on in a short time and you get the feeling it's somehow drug related. We're also getting rumors from the drug- gies there's some heavy shit coming down the pike. There's a general increase in drug activity."

"I suggest you follow the money trail with Reed," Chic said. "See what you can find out about his business dealings. What car lots, what pawnshops and other businesses he frequented. Does he own the business, finance the business or what exactly is his connection and interest in the businesses he regularly called on? Who's handling that business now? This should lead to a pattern of behavior that will eventually lead to his contacts. Somewhere in his contacts are the people who have the safe. When we find them, we'll solve this mystery."

"Heath, I see the waitress coming with my five dollar meal. I guess we better hold this for a minute and eat our breakfast."

"Yeah, besides I need some more coffee to get my brain working this morning."

"What? You have an overactive weekend?" asked Chic.

"I wish I had," replied Heath. Both men seemed to perk up with a little food in their stomachs. Heath picked up the conversation.

"Chic, the other problem we're getting wind of is that the Mexican gangs may be fighting over the North Florida territory. We know that the drug traffic is out of Mexico, but up to now, they've confined their fight to Mexico. We can only hope that the carnage we see in Mexico doesn't play out here."

"Anything is possible, Heath. The Mexican gangs have no regard for life and there's really nothing stopping this type of violence from rearing its head here in Fort Walton. If they start killing judges and law enforcement officers along with their families, there's going to be hell to pay. Hopefully they fear us enough that they'll confine their turf battle to Mexico. Finding out how the drug cartel is related to the safe and to the murders may be impossible. That fast and furious operation of the ATF lets us know that even the feds haven't cracked the Mexican cartels or crime syndicates in America. In fact, the present policies of the federal government amount to an invitation to the cartels to openly move their operations to US soil. I believe they see a clear opening based on their lack of fear of our commitment to stop them."

"Good way to start off a Monday, don't you think?" Heath laughed as he slapped Chic on the back. "All we need now is for the drug gangs from Mexico, who have God only knows how much money at their disposal, to conclude they can buy judges, police officers and politicians in the Panhandle. On the one hand, they start killing and with the other hand, they hold out money for cooperation. I tell you, Chic—I believe our country is at a point where we're now vulnerable to this kind of pressure. Under pressure, many good people will sell their souls."

"You're right about that," Chic said. "I had a crook tell me one time that I would be surprised at how cheap it was to bribe people. He would know because he bribed people often enough. I don't believe we're there yet, but I'm not sure how well we'll respond should the Mexican gangs decide to move their killing and bribery to the US. We can expect them to test our country's commitment to law and order."

"This case worries me because it has the earmark of big money," Heath said. "That means to me that drugs are at the bottom. That John Doe killing could be seen as the beginnings of a drug turf battle. Problem is how to relate the drug trade to the money laundering operation, which I believe is involved."

"Gets my blood circulating on Monday morning, talking about blood and guts with you," replied Chic. "What about Suzy Beal? The one who escaped from Gertrude's house. Does she know anything?"

"Not really. If it weren't so serious, it would be right funny. She can't really identify anybody, but they know who she is by now. Suzy's picture has been plastered all over the news, so they know who she is, where she works, where she lives and that she's into group sex. The news loves this kind of story."

"I had a call on my answering machine from her," said Chic. "She wants to talk to me. Thinks she needs my help. Do you think I ought to call her?"

"Well, might not be a bad idea, Chic. The two perps might think she knows something, so she could be in danger. How well do you know her?"

"Not well. I think I have seen her before, but we've never been officially introduced. She works at the college as a physical education instructor. She probably heard I sometimes work with the police. She also knows I'm involved in the music department. I think I'll call her back and see what she wants. I'll keep you posted. Let me know when you have some more info on Reed and the safe. Put what resources you can on getting Reed's financial records and put some guys on running down his daily contacts. Find out everything you can about his business and this should lead us to who replaced Reed."

"How's that going to solve the other murder cases, Chic? The chief is going to want to know and he's going to need an excuse to devote resources to this before he'll agree to the idea. The chief has a point. We don't need this information to connect the ninjas to the Reed murders. How do we connect the cases?"

"The connection is in the safe, Heath. The connection has to be through Reed, not the ninjas. We'll find the connection through those who have a nexus with Reed."

Chic looked at his watch and realized he was running a little late for his first patient at his office. "Heath, I'm running a little late to the office. We'll pick this conversation up later. Now, don't forget to pay for my breakfast. I don't need them chasing me down the street."

Chic got into his red Ford Mustang convertible, let the top down to soak up the sun and with his blond hair flopping in the breeze headed toward his office to meet with clients. He was thinking about the problems of the day, but Suzy kept creeping into his mind. *Perhaps*, he thought, *there must be some sexual connotation in my mind between the fresh air and Suzy. Not an unpleasant thought. Suzy was a fine-looking redheaded woman who oozed sex from every pore in her agile body. Well, a little wild. No, a lot wild.* The story of her flight from the scene of the crime, naked and vulnerable, was the funniest thing he had ever heard. *A girl with that much spunk couldn't be all bad!* Chic began to think that his call to duty wouldn't be completely unpleasant. He realized he was looking forward to their conversation.

The next day, Chic had an appointment to meet with one of the voice teachers of the university to help prepare him for his performance at an upcoming event in Mobile, Alabama. As luck would have it, Suzy had a class at about the same time, so Chic managed to be waiting for her outside her classroom.

Chic observed through the glass pane in the door that Suzy was indeed agile. She had a quick smile, the physique of a dancer and a face made for the stage. He was impressed. *Was this just simply his animal response to beauty or did she have gravitas? No, I think I'll just go with describing her as a stunning beauty.* He knew from the college rumor mill that in addition to that sharp body, she had a sharp wit and keen mind. By the time Suzy dismissed the class and opened the door leading to the hall, Chic had already decided that this girl was something special in spite of her reputation for sport sex.

Suzy looked up at Chic with surprise as she almost ran into him when she came through the door.

She gathered herself. "Wow! Sorry, I almost knocked you down with the door."

"I'm the one who should be sorry," said Chic. "I'm afraid I got a little transfixed watching you through the window and just didn't move fast enough. I'm Chic and I'm here to answer the call of a distressed maiden. I hope you don't mind my casual tone about this serious problem. We've never met officially, so I'm Chic Sparks and I assume you're Suzy Beal."

"Yes, I am. I recognized you from a concert I attended recently. By the way, I'm very impressed with your voice. It's a real pleasure to meet you."

"Thank you, Suzy. I must admit that I'm impressed with your gymnastic ability. If you don't mind my saying so, I'm very impressed with your escape from the murder scene. Very few people could have gotten out of that situation alive."

"I can assure you that I don't like to think about it. I hope you don't mind my calling on you even though you and I are basically strangers."

"Why don't we go down the street and get some coffee and talk about this in private?" he suggested.

They got into Chic's Mustang and drove to the nearest Waffle House, which just happened to be one of Chic's favorite hangouts. Halfway there, Chic thought about how ridiculous it was to bring this good-looking gal to a Waffle House. As Chic pulled into the parking lot, he realized that he can't deny his red-neck roots as a law enforcement officer, so Waffle House it was.

Seated in the back corner of the Waffle House, Suzy and Chic clearly struck a contrast with the usual patrons.

It crossed Suzy's mind that without being too stuck on herself, she and Chic made a damn fine-looking couple. Waffle House or the Waldorf Astoria, she would feel rather cozy seated with this good-looking guy. Suzy couldn't help but think that in her days as sport sex specialist, she had never had the privilege of having a man with the x-factor, which Chic surely had. *Sex as a sport,* she mused, *had gotten her in plenty of trouble. Was it time to change her life?* As she sipped her coffee, Suzy had to fight the thought that in the presence of this good-looking stud with a pure animal sex appeal, maybe she could just delay her transformation for a spell. Suzy let out a petite sigh as she sipped her coffee, thinking that there was no need to do today what she could put off until tomorrow.

Chic, for his part, thought that the sigh was a sign of frustration with the circumstances in which Suzy found herself. In a way, he was right, of course, but he missed the real circumstance of her frustration. *Can a trained psychologist be blamed for misreading the true thoughts of a woman? In particular, this vixen?*

Chic began his inquisition. "I talked to Detective Heath Moore about this case, so I'm at least familiar with all the information the police have. I can understand that you might be worried that the crooks might have some interest in you as the only witness to the murders. Have you been contacted by anyone, received any threats, felt like you've been followed or had any other unusual thing happen since the night of the murders?"

"Not really. My name and picture have been in the newspapers. I've been seen on TV. I get a lot of interesting looks from the staff and students at the school. Many of the staff feel like I'm a bad influence at a Christian school, but it's a 'cast the first stone' sort of thing. I get the impression that some people look at me like a freak or a loose woman or as an easy mark, but I haven't gotten the feeling that the killers are after me. I understand that everybody knows why I was at the scene of the crime and I'll have to live with that. Chic, nobody likes to have their own little pleasure palaces exposed to the world. My real concern and the reason I need your help is that my logic tells me that the killers are still worried about what I saw. While I've not been threatened, I don't feel safe."

Chic studied Suzy as she talked and was at least satisfied that her concerns were real and not based on some emotional, maudlin reaction. He was impressed that this woman was able to handle this life-changing event with a real degree of reflection and with both feet on the ground, so to speak.

"Suzy, why don't you tell me the whole story about the night of the murders?"

Suzy complied and repeated the entire story about what she saw and heard that night. She got a little perverse pleasure in telling Chic all the details of the sexual part of the story.

Chic listened intently and when Suzy finished, Chic concluded, "You know a little more than you think. You saw that the two men, whom you believe committed the murders, were white and not black. From the way they handled themselves, they seemed to be good old Southern boys. You know their relative sizes. One was tall and the other was short. You think the taller guy seemed to be in charge. The problem is that we don't know what the crooks think you may know. What they think you know is more important than what you actually know. They can't be sure how much you know about the actual shooting.

"What they do know is everything about you. They've seen you in the news. They know where you live and where you work. You're therefore vulnerable at least on two levels: One, they may think you know something that endangers them. Second, they're men and therefore you're vulnerable as a good-looking woman with active sexual interests. The two together clearly put your life in danger.

"I hope you're not offended by my reference to your sexual activity. As a clinical psychologist, I'm kind of familiar with the sexual patterns you've described. It's not my job to condemn you or to preach to you. I think you want me to help you with some survival skills and I'm happy to oblige. As a clinical psychologist, I have to tell you that you were having way too much fun giving me all the sexual detail of the night. Naughty, naughty."

"Chic," said Suzy with a Cheshire cat smile on her face, "I have to be honest with you. I don't like my life being exposed like this. Yeah, I actually did enjoy filling you in on that. I have enough sense to know that while I really want to hide this kind of activity, the world wants to hear the details of sexual exploits. I can say that no matter what choices I've made, I was simple minded enough to think I could do all this in secret. I don't like my life being an open book, but now it is. I believe I need your help and that's what I'm thinking about. Being honest, I have to confess that I find you to be quite an interesting man, but I'll make every effort to behave myself. I promise not to rape you."

"I appreciate your openness," Chic said. "This is one of those situations where if I refuse to make a pass at you, I'm somehow rejecting you as a person, or if I make a pass at you, I'm taking advantage of the situation. So let me give you my honest opinion, which is that I find you a very attractive person and one I actually would like to get to know better. I confess that it's tempting to think of the marvelous pleasure to partake of your passion in any form. I hope you don't mind if I use some self-control and direct my attention to saving your life and maybe in the process getting to know you better."

"You know, Chic, that's a line I've never heard before. In other words, you want us to act like adults first and simply get to know one another. I actually think I like that idea. It's a deal. I don't think I have to confess that I don't have a long history of deep, personal relationships."

"Well," he said, "now that we know we both have weaknesses and have to control the very human temptations of the flesh, let's get down to business."

Suzy grabbed Chic's hand, looked him in the eyes with her very best smile and said, "For a girl who's used her charms to manipulate men most of her life, I find it very refreshing to be handled so smoothly." With a final squeeze, Suzy straightened up, put her hand in her lap and in a business-like fashion said, "Shoot."

"Okay, what kind of training have you had with a gun?"

"None."

"With your background, I'm sure you've had some physical defense training. What's your level of competency in the martial arts?"

"Just basic. I've actually taught some of the basic defense measures for women in my classes, but I could use some training in lethal techniques."

"We're going to leave here and get you outfitted over at Money Mizer's Pawnshop with a personal firearm. Then we're going to the firing range. I'll get you lined up with one of my ranger buddies to bring you up to speed on all the lethal moves you'll need. Then we're going to your house to make sure we have in place all the defensive measures you'll need there. At the pawn-shop, we'll get you outfitted with the best pepper spray and anything else we think you'll need. For the time being, we're going to assume that either the killers or some pervert is going to attack you. Most likely this will be at your home, but you must be prepared at all times, especially when you're shopping. Anytime you're alone, you must assume that you're being followed. We'll school you in the necessary observation skills, although from what I've seen, you're very keen in that area. Basic alertness is something people are born with, but we can enhance that skill."

"Okay, Chic. Let's get out of here and get to work."

As they walked toward Chic's Mustang, Chic couldn't help but smile at the thought of working with this girl for a few weeks. Great minds think alike and so it should be no surprise that Suzy had exactly the same thought. Suzy had to turn her head so Chic couldn't see her expression, which she knew had to look like a little girl who had just found her favorite lost doll.

Chic couldn't stop his mind from pondering the nature of God and man. God was no stranger to the sexual appetites of man and beast. God had created all living creatures with a strong sexual desire as a necessary component of life itself. Chic, looking at this aspect of the human condition from the viewpoint of God, the creator, in spite of some of the Old Testament teachings, could believe that God's attitude about sex was far more lax than man's viewpoint. Chic reviewed the sexual appetites of God's greatest prophets, which he concluded ran the whole gambit of sexual behavior. Chic thought of King David who had a man killed so he could possess his wife. In spite of David's sexual exploits, the Bible reported that he was favored in God's view.

Chic viewed the Bible as teaching that God created man, as well as this entire universe, but it didn't tell the specific method of that creation. God would expect man to use his brain and believe what he saw since there could be no conflict between God's creation and his Word. From that point of view, there would be no conflict between all of his laws of nature and his Word. The only conflict was whether man believed God created the universe he saw via the laws of creation he put in place. The heavens told of the wonders of God and arguing over the age of the universe from this viewpoint was childish. How could anyone ignore the facts of the age of the universe and believe one was not a Christian unless he thought earth was only five thousand years old?

The human sex drive and method of reproduction reinforced Chic's view that man arose from the animal kingdom in the fashion of other creations. Humans, without some self-control, act "animal like" in their sexual habits. History and experience, as well as religion, urged man to rise above his animal nature and control his passions within the confines of accepted mores. Suzy had given in to her base nature but was clearly a soul seeking redemption. He wouldn't cast the first stone.

Chic smiled to himself at the smallness of our minds when we believe that a creative process taking billions of years is somehow inconsistent with a perfect God who has no beginning and no end. *God is not bound to a belief that everything had to be created in six days of twenty-four hours each. Nor is God confined to a limited view of man's sexual appetite.* It occurred to Chic that this vision was capable of expanding his own view of sex.

Chic smiled as he considered how this young lady he only met a few short hours ago, without saying a word, had managed to rattle his concept of human sexual behavior.

— 11 —

Early October in the Panhandle of Florida is a delightful experience. Most of the tourists have gone home and the locals are able to easily move about and get to their favorite eating establishments. The long lines are gone. Unless there is a tropical storm on the horizon, the sky is a clear blue and there is just enough coolness in the air to give the oysters that special zest.

How wonderful it was to be alive on a day like today, especially on a yacht, feeling the cool air course over your face. It was close enough to the summer to remember the heat and not cold enough to remind you of the coming winter. Sailing along on a blue-bird day with a little coolness in the air, the snow-white beaches in fact looked like snow. The sand there was unique in the world. There were about two hundred miles of pure white sand ground into perfect little spheres through millions of years of grinding down mountains in the Smoky Mountain range, which at one time was higher than the Colorado peaks.

Boss couldn't help but be delighted at the sheer pleasure he felt as his fifty-foot yacht, *Amadee*, coursed around Perdido Key on the way to the Gulf of Mexico. Victor was an adequate captain and could handle the boat with ease. With the caterpillar diesel engine and bow thrusters, they could move in and out of dock with ease.

Boss had a little sailor in his blood and from time to time would help man the fifty-foot sailboat in local races. The *Amadee* was more of a cruising yacht than a racer. It was a boat built for the northern sea. Very stable in rough going. The boat was at ease in thirty knots of wind.

His favorite race was from Pensacola, Florida, to Isla Mujeres, Mexico, in May of each year. Boss was a white-water guy and loved the heavy sailing conditions. While he liked his motor yacht, he preferred the *Amadee*. A good sailboat road the waves better and could take a real beating. If he was going to be in heavy weather, he needed to be in a sailboat like the *Amadee.*

Boss sat at the helm, feet on the boat rail, cigar in his mouth and his mind in another universe. Boss could feel the direction of the wind and the movement of the boat hitting the waves at the correct angle helped guide his hands on the helm. His favorite experience on the *Amadee* was that time when they sailed alongside a pod of whales for an hour. He could still see the baby whale suckling his mother as they moved in rhythm with the pod. Occasionally the bull whale would surface with his big eye directly pointed at Boss. There was a clear warning to back off from the pod. In that universe, his mind saw no problems, only pleasure.

What is it, he wondered, *that moved a guy like himself from a young kid who tried to make a few pennies to where he now was? The events of life had led him intractably to this captain's chair on this boat. Had he a choice in the decisions he had made along the way or had some greater power preordained his life? He had accepted every challenge that had come his way. He was not a passive observer of life. Did he ordain his life of crime?* As he allowed his mind to wonder, he could not deny that he loved the excitement of his life. He loved the money. He loved the power. He loved the intrigue of it all. He couldn't deny that he loved the power he had over life and death. He loved the game and his ability to deceive the common people. Being an engaging sociopath, what Boss did not feel was the pains of conscience for the evil he had done. The necessary death he had caused was purely a business decision. Whatever decisions he had made were necessary for his success. People with their hangups and inefficiencies were unwanted impediments to achieving his goals.

The reverie was broken with the sound of an approaching tender. *Time for work. Back to the real world. Back to the universe of pain and the pleasure of business.*

"Ahoy, George Currier here. May I come aboard?"

Boss reeled in the main sail and the genoa. He could accomplish this with toggle switches at the helm. Boss motioned for George to come along the side where the ladder was located. "Throw Victor your line," he said.

Victor got the line and George climbed the ladder and came aboard. The tender line was fed out aft and Boss raised the genoa and got under way, towing the tender.

George and Boss took a seat in the open helm area and Victor took the yacht at a slow pace along the coastline. He engaged the autopilot and joined George and Boss. They got out the small rods and trolled along for king mackerel.

"George, my name is Boss. Never call me by any other name. You don't need to know my real name and if you know it, never write it down and never say it aloud. You've been with the organization long enough to know the routine. We follow the chain of command. Your immediate manager is Victor. You see Victor, Victor sees me, I talk to the Big Boss. It is necessary to maintain these strict firewalls. It protects everybody up and down the line."

"You got it, Boss," said George. "I was briefed in New Mexico before I came here. I did the same job in New Mexico that Reed did for you here. It looks like he got a little sloppy and maintained some incriminating records. He probably skimmed some cash from the organization."

"That's right, George. That happened on my watch and it will not happen again. Records are kept by headquarters in the gold and drug operations. After each monthly report, the money and records leave here, except for the operating accounts. There should be no local records. If we need back up, then you let me know and I'll get the info. We were fortunate enough to recover the safe before anyone gained access. Those records are now history. As we all know, every human activity leaves some kind of trace. For example, Reed had certain regular customers he called on several times over the course of a month. When you lend money and make collections, everybody at those locations knows you. Should the police retrace the business activity of Thomas Reed, they'll establish a pattern. They'll find out who you are, George. We can't avoid that. In our lending operation with the pawnshops, title pawn and used car lots, these are handled through an operating loan company controlled by Victor. You will deal with these customers as their broker.

"You will therefore come in as a new competitor taking over Reed's last business and renewing the loans. New company name, new identity. As for the drug side, you'll use your own men. So, it's important that you and Victor don't become drinking pals. You don't need to be seen together. There should be no visual or written connection between the legitimate business and off-line business.

"When we meet, it will normally be on the yacht. You'll get a message left on your answering machine three days before the meeting only stating the time. If there's a change in the meeting location, the phone message will also leave a code, which you'll have for each of our locations.

"George, I believe Victor has briefed you on our area of operation. You'll take care of the pawnshops, pawn title companies, gold-buying schemes, car lots and drug business. You'll have to reestablish the business. I need also to mention that Reed had a car lot and a payroll check-cashing business, which he owned. We are not to deal with those businesses at all. No loans, no contact.

"Let's talk about the drug business. I'm sure your experience in New Mexico qualifies you as our expert in this area."

"You're right about that," said George. "We've had some fights between the Mexican gangs, but so far the Sinaloa have been able to keep the Zeta under control. There has been some head banging going on, but they've kept their fighting mainly in Mexico. I understand they may be moving the fight into this area. I can tell you that my man knows how to handle the Mexicans. I have contacted the Sinaloa and they're working on the problem. If we crack heads in the US, I'll use my boys. If it's done in Mexico, Sinaloa will do it. You may see some activity soon. We've identified two or three of the Zeta and my boys are taking care of business as we speak."

"Cover your ass, George. Make sure there's no one left to tell the tale."

"Boss, you can go to the bank on that one."

Victor, who had been listening to this point, asserted himself. "Boss, while we're reviewing the whole operation, we probably need to go over the money flow. It does vary a little bit from region to region."

"Sure, Victor, you've got the floor."

"As we all know, the money for large transactions comes by check or money orders from one of the charitable companies controlled by Boston. Money that we make off loans goes to whatever company is assigned by Boston. The money we make on drug operations and the gold business is either sent to Boston or kept here to fund the gold business and to make the smaller loans. We also wash some of the money through the bogus mortgage business using numerous banks in the area. We normally stick with small local banks. I'm the contact with banks. Since the gold business is a cash operation, this is where we wash most of the cash we generate locally."

The meeting continued for another forty-five minutes until Boss was satisfied that George was a vast improvement over Reed. George was a man from the shadows. Reed sought attention. Boss had a reason to play his role as a popular businessman. The rest of his organization couldn't stand the light of day. While nothing is perfect, his operation was as compartmentalized as possible, considering the necessity of controlling the flow of money. Even among thieves there has to be control in place.

"Start the motor, Victor!" shouted Boss. "I'm ready to catch and grill some king mackerel," he said as he headed for the fishing poles.

Later that night, an ordinary white van carrying three well-dressed Mexicans pulled out from Jim's used car lot and headed out to US Highway 98. A block away, an old Ford 150 pickup pulled onto Highway 98 ahead of the white van. As both vehicles moved toward the east, an old Crown Vic pulled out behind the white van.

In the white van, the occupants were laughing about the coup they had just pulled off. They had managed to take a big drug deal away from the Sinaloa without a hitch. "Fuck the Sinaloa," said the driver. "They're dealing with the Zeta now." The two in the backseat were not listening. They were too busy snorting cocaine.

They had conquered the world! What could possible go wrong now?

As the three vehicles approached a dark area along the highway, they found no traffic on the road to impede their plan. The truck, traveling about four hundred feet in front, came to a sudden stop in front of the van. The driver of the van hit his brakes while at the same time a Crown Vic came along the left side of the van. Before the three Mexicans in the van could react, hails of shots were fired from the passenger side of the Crown Vic and from the truck in front. Before the van could come to a stop, the three Mexicans were dead. The van was still slowly rolling as the truck was leaving the scene. The Crown Vic stopped only long enough to let out two occupants who quickly took control of the white van. One took the wheel and reentered Highway 98 as if nothing had happened.

The next day, the paper reported the event as a gang-related murder. Authorities recovered the white van containing three headless bodies from a creek that crossed a lonely dirt road near Ponce de Leon. The headless men had no identification and the van turned out to be stolen. There were enough drugs in the van to lead authorities to the conclusion that this was a drug deal gone badly, but they found no sign of money.

The Sinaloa left a clear message to the drug dealers in the Panhandle. If you get your drugs from anybody else you may lose your head. Leaving the drugs in the van let the dealers know that this wasn't a robbery or the act of some drug crazed nut, but was a carefully planned assassination.

Two days later the three heads turned up neatly packed in a special delivery box at the compound of a Zeta principal. The message was clear in Monterey, Mexico and in Fort Walton Beach, Florida: "Back off!"

In Florida, the DEA and drug cops were on high alert. It was clear that a drug war was going on, but it was not clear that the rash of killings were related to that war. The intent was to redirect the efforts of the police away from the detailed investigation of Reed's contacts sequestered by Chic and direct them toward the drug scene.

It was clear that beheading was a common strategy used in the battle between Mexican drug cartels. There was nothing in the Reed deaths and Gertrude's death that looked like the Mexican cartels were involved. Of course, Randall Moss claimed he was the hired killer, but no one actually believed that.

Across the street from a small used car lot in Fort Walton, two men sat in a white van waiting for the two men on duty that night to close the pawn-shop. These two men in the pawnshop were the drug dealers who bought their drugs from the Zetas. It was already dark and there were no other people in the area. Traffic was light. A sleeping gas canister was carefully placed in their car with a radio-activated device to trigger its release. As soon as the two pawnshop men shut the door to their car, the device was activated and the two men were quickly disabled. The white van advanced across the street and the two men were quickly loaded into the van.

The white van headed toward the inter-coastal waterway where their twenty-eight-foot fishing boat was waiting. A plastic bag was placed over the heads of the disabled men and their trials on earth were swiftly ended. The two lifeless bodies were loaded onto the fishing boat, which promptly headed for the open gulf.

It was a good night for wet work. A dark, hazy and moonless night with no breeze to stir the gulf, so the water was totally calm. Not even a ripple. You could spit in the gulf and watch the centric circles ripple along the surface.

Only a gentle swell reminded you that you were in the Gulf of Mexico. The boat, rigged for bottom fishing, trolled out about ten miles before idling the two diesels.

The two bodies were prepared for permanent residence in Davy Jones's Locker. Their torsos were opened and weights were permanently attached to the bodies. The two naked bodies were thrown into the gulf. Sharks and sea creatures of all kinds would consume virtually every part of the bodies. Time and seawater would dissolve the weights.

For this time-tested crew, cleaning the boat to remove all sign of the bodies was no worse than cleaning up after a night of bottom fishing. As one of the men cleaned the boat, the other did some bottom fishing. They followed their normal routine and when they had caught their limit, they returned to the dock where their boat normally birthed.

The men gave the boat another thorough cleaning including a steam bath.

Still pumped up from the night's activities, the men stopped by their favorite breakfast joint and then went home for a little rest. They were satisfied men who had completed a successful night's work.

— 12 —

Gold was a wonderful thing to Boss. It was beautiful, it never rusted and its supply was limited, therefore making it valuable. If there was anything that was permanent, it was gold. It was nice to hold in his hand and women loved it. If it had a weakness, it was that most women he knew were more attracted to drugs than gold. Boss knew that the drug dealer was easily spotted in a bar. Look and see what man has the most blonde women around him and there was your dealer. He also had to admit that the dealers usually displayed a lot of gold.

In his business, gold played a central role. It was a marvelous way to launder cash. He used the cash supply derived from drugs and other off-line operations to buy the gold. You take the gold to a smelter who pays you coins, bullion or gives you credit, any of which can be used in the future. Or he gives you a check. In any event, what comes out the other side is basically clean.

The washed money can then be sent to headquarters where it is funneled into various controlled charitable or church corporations that become the lender in legitimate mortgage transactions. The negotiable commercial paper is then sold on the open market. The money that the various companies get when they sell the legitimate mortgage in the open market is then lost in the daisy-chain maze of corporations, none of which were any more solid than the morning haze. Keeping track of all the activity was the fundamental weakness of the system. Record keeping leads to discovery and no record keeping leads to certain theft.

Ah! The beauty of it all gave Boss a feeling matched only by the all-consuming pleasure of a beautiful and submissive woman.

Boss entered his walk-in closet, went to a small safe, turned the key and dialed in the combination. Inside, he pressed the back of the safe, which was actually a pressure plate that when pressed released the hydraulic door in the equipment room located off a nearby hallway. When the hydraulic door opened, Boss was then able to enter the anteroom where the vault door was located.

The door would slide open and unless you were in the room with the air compressor, you would never know there was a door there that led to the vault.

The house had been cleverly designed to make the secret space. The entire vault room was protected with an inner and outer sheet of one-inch-high strength steel with six feet of poured reinforced concrete on all six surfaces. The entire safe area was fully insulated from fire. Once inside, there was essentially a small bank vault with a high-grade vault door with a timer that could only be reset from inside the vault. Boss had also provided self-protection features that he could control from the inside. Aside from Boss, only Victor knew of this safe. For decoy purposes, Boss had a smaller safe that was easily discoverable. He kept enough money in that safe to convince any robber that it was in fact the main safe.

From inside, he counted out one million in cash, which would cover the gold-buying operation for a normal month. Janice and her boyfriend, Stan, would use about a hundred thousand weekly in their own direct gold-buying operation. The rest would be used to buy gold from the dealers at pawnshops and flea markets. It was their job to take the gold to the smelters and then account to Victor. The operation returned the original million monthly, along with an average net profit of over 25 percent. He and Victor were confident they could control these two. If the volume or profit varied much from their expectation, some other couple would take their place.

Boss locked the money in a couple of old suitcases, which he loaded in his old twenty-foot fishing boat. As usual, he timed the trips for thirty minutes before sunrise so he would look like any other fisherman headed out for a day's fishing. Dressed to play the part, cup of coffee in hand, he headed out toward Valparaiso. He normally met Victor at the channel marker out of Valparaiso and that was the plan this morning. After an innocent radio check, they came together near the Eglin facility where the suitcases were passed over to Victor and Victor gave his packages to Boss. After setting up the next meeting, the boats separated, each to their separate locations in opposite directions.

There was no need for a review on the other end of the transaction since Victor would repay the basic loan, which Boss's company had made to Victor's loan company. The difference in the profit would be given to Boss the same way as today. That money would be deposited and used to pay for a loan made to Boss's company, which would be processed back to Boss in the form of a fully documented loan.

Boss would also keep some of the washed money locally and add it to cash money that was washed through the bogus home loan businesses.

Victor met Janice and Stan later that morning for breakfast at Joe and Eddies, the world's best breakfast for the money. Victor thought of Janice and Stan as a delightful couple, charming and very competent in the gold trade. He had followed them closely enough to know they were trustworthy. They were happy to be making a decent living.

He had found Janice working at a Waffle House. He was impressed as hell by her ability to handle the public and she was actually a good-looking woman, a rare breed for the Waffle House gang. A rare find indeed.

When he first tried to get her to come to work for him, she thought he was just after a piece of ass. Not a bad idea, in fact. He put a check mark in his mind that if he ever had to dispose of her, he was going to get a piece of ass first.

Well, you couldn't blame Janice for thinking that a guy offering her a job making a couple of thousand a week was full of shit. After all, she had never known anybody who actually made more than four hundred dollars a week in her life. She and Stan had taken the lessons, learned all about testing and buying gold and everything Victor had told her turned out to be true. The money she was now making was like a gift from heaven.

Janice had no concept of the part she was playing in the grand scheme of the criminal enterprise that emanated from Boston. Her limited experience as well as her basic innocence of the darkness of the criminal mind rendered her blind to anything more than the small world in which she moved.

There were times when Victor coveted her innocence, but these moments were rare blips on his otherwise guiltless life. Victor rarely suffered from the drug of reflective thinking. He didn't have time for that kind of psychosocial bull crap.

"Where are you going to start tomorrow morning?" asked Victor.

Janice answered, as she was the voice of the team, "We're going to be in Pensacola and Mobile this week. Stan will be in charge of buying gold from our normal customers and I'll be in charge of buying from individuals. We have our usual helpers. I'm sure we'll need to see you two or three times this week to give you product and to get more funds."

"Fine," said Victor. "Call me and we'll meet in Pensacola or either in Crestview. Be careful and make sure you keep the security detail I've assigned to you close at hand."

"Sure thing," said Janice. "It would be nice if you could do this business without cash, but people want cash, not a check. You can bet we won't get far away from our security detail."

"Good," said Victor. "Can't be too careful. There are too many crooks out there. You really have to watch out for those druggies. If they're out of money, they'll kill anybody to get money for their drugs. It's really terrible that we don't seem to be able to slow down the use of drugs in this country. I just don't know what this world is coming to."

"I'm glad you feel that way, Victor," said Janice. "I can't imagine why anyone would get involved in the drug trade. Sometimes I think the world is going to hell in a hand basket. Look at all the killings going on here between Fort Walton and Pensacola. The way it's going, we're going to be like Mexico here in the Panhandle."

"It's a rotten show," said Victor. "Just be careful and watch your back at all times."

"You know, Victor, Stan and I really appreciate the opportunity you've given us to make a decent living. When we first started, I thought you were just shooting us a line, but you've proved to be a man of your word."

"Janice, you have to know that we look after our own. We appreciate honest and hard work. As long as you play straight with us, you and Stan have job security. One thing we demand is honesty. Cash money is tempting. Don't give in to that temptation." Victor gave this instruction with a smile, but as his eyes locked on Janice and then on Stan, they told a different story. Janice and Stan displayed their survival skills, for they got the correct message.

"Now, get out of here and get to work," said Victor. Who could resist patting Janice on her ass as she followed Stan out the door? Not Victor.

Victor paid the bill and moved out the door slowly as he admired Janice's sassy ass as she sauntered at a perky pace to her car. His mind flipped to the image he had envisioned of Suzy's heavenly body. He envisioned what an out-of-the-world experience it would be to get Suzy and Janice in bed together. It certainly would meet his definition of space pussy.

Victor had to fight his weakness for women, which sometimes turned into a burning compulsion. Suzy might know something and might not, but Boss had given him specific instructions not to harm her or have any contact with her. Boss tried to explain how any action toward her would mathematically increase the chances of Boss's discovery. Whatever she knew, Boss told him, was far less damaging than going after her would be.

Victor couldn't quite follow Boss's reasoning on this one. What could be the harm? When he got through with her, his itch would be scratched and she would be gone. Nobody would ever find her, so what's the problem? Not even Boss would be any the wiser.

— 13 —

While Victor was doing his thing, George was also on the road taking care of business. He had his boys out taking care of deliveries and collections for drugs. The dealers were still in place, although two of them were contacted by the Zeta cartel and the one that actually bought drugs from them had been dealt with.

Chopping off heads proved to be effective. He had received word that the Zetas and Sinaloa had more or less worked out the territorial problems, essentially dividing the United States into protected territories. Everyone knew that drugs originated from many sources in the United States and no single cartel could gain total dominion. Too many varieties of drugs on the market and too many ways to meet that demand. George knew that a druggie could always find something to zap his central nervous system. George knew he had a form of job security—his ability to supply and disperse the favorite drug of choice being the main part of that security. George was particularly fond of the enforcement side of his job.

He really liked the part where he lopped off heads. It got a lot of publicity and created a lot of random fear. It made his job easier. He didn't have to worry at this point about the Zeta. He especially liked his touch with the two dealers who had bought their drugs from the Zeta. These had simply disappeared without a trace. Some sharks had been particularly happy to feast on those boys' body parts.

George was on his way to meet attorney Albert Barnes at Wetzel's in Mobile, Alabama. George had heard a lot about the seafood in the Panhandle and he had not been disappointed. He had tried many of the best places, but this would be his first shot at Wetzel's.

George had made himself familiar with this operation and knew Victor had a close relationship with Albert Barnes. He liked the overall scheme, although to him it had too many moving parts. The scheme was effective at washing a good deal of money, but not the large amounts you could wash by other methods. Whatever—it was good on a local basis to provide Boss money for the local team. His job today was to deliver seventy-five thousand dollars cash to Albert. Albert would add this to the cash in his safe and slowly feed this money into his trust account which would provide the essential protection from discovery.

Victor kept close tabs on this money and had determined that Albert was at least an honest crook. Their concern was his drug use. Addiction to drugs and gambling led to destruction in this or any other business. George had a duel job this day and that was to warn Albert as well as to analyze Albert in terms of his reliability.

Albert already had a table at the agreed upon location. When George arrived at Wetzel's, he was exactly on time and Albert was waiting for him. Neither man had trouble recognizing the other from the photographs they had.

George tried the raw oysters, gumbo and the fried snapper. Man, they didn't have anything like this in New Mexico. George had already decided that the Panhandle was the place for him. He liked the women, liked the food, liked the weather, liked the pure white sand and business was good. He was forming the conclusion that New Mexico was more dangerous than here, but he had not been here long enough to draw a final conclusion about that. The people in the Panhandle were certainly nicer. On the other hand, he had concluded that you really shouldn't underestimate some of these red necks.

"Albert," said George, "when's your next closing?"

"Probably Thursday or Friday of next week. I now have funding for that loan, which will be two hundred fifty thousand dollars," replied Albert. "Who's going to handle this, you or Victor?"

"Well, I'm sure Victor will be at the closing. He usually makes sure the sellers and purchasers are there. I may help him from time to time, but Victor is still in charge. I guess you can call me a delivery boy."

George was watching Albert carefully and noticed Albert was a little jittery. His eyes were too jumpy and his general demeanor was too hyper.

"Albert," said George, looking him straight in the eye, "what is it?

Cocaine, meth, prescription drugs? Could be marijuana… One reason I'm here today is to make it clear to you that you must stay off the drugs. We don't need you out of control, running your mouth flashing too much money around."

"George, I'm not a druggie. I'm a little uptight today—had way too much coffee."

"Look, you're talking to me now and I think I know a thing or two about drugs. It's bad enough to have a problem, but when you get into denial, that makes it worse. I'm telling you this for your own good. You need to get your head on straight. If we're going to stay in business with you, you're going to have to clean up your act."

"Now look here, George, if you knew me better, you would know that I'm not high. I'll admit that sometimes I might get high, but I keep it under control. Right now I'm as clean as a hound's tooth."

"Have it your way, Albert, but make no mistake. If your drug use interferes with our business, you'll be out. Don't let that happen."

"Look, George, I know you're new, but Victor knows that he can trust me. This business was my idea. I sold this idea to Victor and he provided the financing, which I appreciate. The business has been good to all of us, so quit worrying. You can bet I'm not going to mess up my gravy train."

"That's fine, Albert. Now let's have another beer and I've got to get back to work."

"What exactly is your line of work?"

"Not that you need to know, but I'm the leg man for Victor's loan company," George said. "That's why I'm here today—bringing the money. If things get out of hand, then I'm what you might call a troubleshooter. You never want to have to see me as a troubleshooter."

"Believe me, George, I plan to stay on your good side."

Later that same night, George reported to Victor that Albert was okay, but that they needed to keep a close eye on his drug use. While Albert's knowledge was limited to only one area of operation, he could start a downward spiral that might lead to Boss.

"Victor, I suggest we bring in new buyers and sellers from out of town and make sure they don't develop any relationship with Albert. We need to change out these people as often as possible. They need to be brought into town as close to the closing time as possible, paid and then taken back out of town that same day."

"I agree," said George. "We do need to be more careful with the buyers and sellers, so I'll initiate that plan immediately."

— 14 —

Chic arranged to meet Suzy at Ken Renfro's office, which was located at a downtown marina on Escambia Bay. Ken had his office there and kept his motor yacht at the marina, only two hundred feet from his office door.

Chic knew women were into this kind of scene: big boat, ocean breeze, pretty building and of course, he had to place himself in that sexy scene. After all, he believed he cut a pretty good image in his sailor boy outfit. *Okay, Chic,* he thought, *cut it out. You can't let this vixen get your mind off your business.*

The minute he saw Suzy slip out of her BMW convertible, dressed in what could possibly pass as her shooting outfit, Chic knew he was the target. Self-control gone, Chic walked over and gave Suzy a big hug that lasted a second or two longer than necessary.

Damn, this girl feels good, he thought. Suzy didn't pull away but leaned in and got her own measure of Chic's body. A true pleasure, she thought.

"Wow," said Suzy, "I've' never been here before. Whose place is this?"

"I thought I might dazzle you a little bit. This is Ken's office and that's his motor yacht over there."

"Probably a good thing I didn't meet this Ken in my younger days," said Suzy. "I might have been swayed by such an ostentatious display of wealth. Can I take a look at the yacht?"

"I'm sure Ken wouldn't object," said Chic. "You don't want me to believe you've grown up and suddenly become demure, do you?"

Suzy punched Chic in the side with her elbow and said, "You know you're just full of crap, don't you? Take me in to meet Ken so I can see his yacht and then we have to get to work. I promise not to proposition Ken—honest."

Chic wasn't so sure that Ken wouldn't proposition Suzy. He was, after all, quite a lady's man. Chic had a fleeting doubt about his own motives for bringing Suzy, a known sexaholic, into the fox's den. *Was he trying to impress Suzy that he had friends in high places or was he just showing off with a beautiful girl on his arm?* As they walked up to Ken's office, Chic decided that he just wanted to show Ken that he too could land a great-looking woman. Chic couldn't help but chuckle at the level of his thinking when in the presence of this charming vixen.

Ken called out, "Come on in, Chic. Now who is this beautiful little lady you have with you? Why don't you just drop her off and go on about your singing somewhere else. I'll take good care of this little lass."

"That's what I'm afraid of," said Chic. "This is Suzy Beal. Suzy, this is Ken Renfro. He's the rascal who owns this office and the yacht I showed you."

"Good to meet you, Suzy," said Ken.

"Likewise," said Suzy.

"Are you the little lady who was caught up in those murders I heard about on TV?" asked Ken.

"One and the same," replied Suzy. "That's a little publicity I could do without."

"From what I've heard, you were lucky to get out alive," said Ken.

"That's right. I got out by the skin of my teeth. I have Chic teaching me how to keep my skin. If I can keep his mind on business, I'm sure he'll do a good job. Have you got time to show me your yacht?" asked Suzy.

"Of course I do. If we can kick Chic off the deck, I might show you my etchings. Of course, I might need a couple of extra guys to help me kick him off the deck, since for a lacy breeches singer, Chic's one tough dude," Ken said as he slapped Chic on the shoulder.

"You could probably do the job," said Chic. "You still sort of look like a football jock to me."

The three continued their friendly banter as Ken gave Chic and Suzy the grand tour. As Chic and Suzy were leaving, Ken told Chic to bring Suzy over to the card game sometime. "Chic, I believe Miss Suzy here could actually wake up those old farts of the Fish House Gang," said Ken.

"Don't hold your breath. I don't think I'll let her near that bunch of lecherous old farts."

"Why not? That might be fun," said Suzy.

"Ah, quit yanking Ken's strings and get in the car. We've got work to do," said Chic.

Chic got in Suzy's convertible and they headed out toward the sheriff's firing range. Suzy did the driving and Chic did the navigating.

"Ken seems like a real nice guy," said Suzy. "Were you showing me off or were you tempting me? I know you had some reason to meet me at his office. Now fess up. Which one?"

After a pause, Chic replied, "Could have been both. In fact, now that you have me cornered, I believe it was both. After all, you're a knock out and it's fun to be seen with you. You might say that my reputation as a he-man is greatly enhanced with you around. I don't really know why I wanted to tempt you with a known lady's man who has lots of money."

Suzy patted Chic on the knee and with her devilish smile said, "I'm very flattered. It's a two-way street. I like being around you and I can tell that the girls at Ken's office were a little jealous. You know, women like to know that the guy they're with piques the interest of other women. At least I do. And since we're not romantically involved, I'm really interested that you wanted to see how I'd react to a real temptation. Are you trying to decide if I'm worth an emotional investment on your part?"

"Now, who's the psychologist here—you or me? Well, hell, Suzy, you and I have this problem. We both can read each other's souls clearly. As you told me before, everybody likes to have his or her own little secrets. Sometimes we fail to understand ourselves, so it's unnerving when somebody understands your secrets better than you do yourself. As to whether or not I was tempting you, I admit that I was."

Suzy didn't need to wait. She already knew the answer. She knew Chic had a case of infatuation and she wanted that infatuation to morph into something more serious. She knew Chic was not into sex as a parlor game or as a sports activity. She had already decided not to lead Chic down that path. The question facing her was whether she was ready to grow up and learn how to respect herself. No man worth his salt would marry a girl like her and share her with the community. She realized that both of them would have to wait for their souls to resolve their individual struggles with the great "what ifs" of life.

Suzy finally replied, "Waiting for the answer is sometimes best for everyone. Even with our power to read each other's souls, we may have to wait for the picture in our souls to clear."

"Let's skip all this parlor chitchat and get serious about your survival. How's the personal combat coming along with my friend Tom?" asked Chic.

"Good. Tom has got me working on my lethal moves and especially those directed at close encounters. He's got me working on some really good moves in case of an attack while I'm in bed or a surprise attack most anywhere in the house. If I don't kill them with that .38 caliber revolver or that razor-sharp knife I have under my pillow, then I'll just rip out their esophagus. I think at this point, I'm very lethal. Just remember that, buddy, if you ever try to hop in my bed at night."

"I can guarantee you that if I hop into your bed, it won't be a surprise. I'm old-fashioned enough to tell you that we hop in together or not at all."

"That was the correct answer."

"Today, we're going through the entire shooting course," Chic said. "We'll use your little pea-picking .38 caliber revolver. We'll practice some fast draw and some close-quarter moves. The idea, of course, is to shoot the intended target, not yourself. If you draw your gun, it must be to kill. Like all this training, the object is to kill. You will put yourself at risk if you only intend to disable or simply run somebody off. A big part of this training is mental. Don't pull your gun unless you have to, but if you do, it must be to kill. Thinking about it will get you killed."

Chic drilled Suzy the rest of the afternoon. This girl was a good marksman and he was totally confident she would kill if it became necessary.

Chic spent the last hour of the session checking out her karate and self-defense moves. Tom was doing a good job teaching her the lethal part of these moves. This girl was an athlete and was totally able to defend herself. Pound for pound, she was as tough as anybody he knew. Any man thinking that this little angel was an easy mark was in for a real surprise.

— 15 —

Boss went through his office, checking with the girls to make sure loans were in their proper stage of development before he took the weekend off for a little trip to Biloxi, Mississippi, on his motor yacht. Once he was certain the documents on the public closing for Monday were in order, he bade the office ado and it was away to the yacht.

Victor and the girls were already on the yacht, which was fully fueled and ready to go. Boss took the helm as they headed out the pass to the gulf, where he quickly got the yacht up to cruising speed. They were taking the outside route in the gulf instead of the inter-coastal route. The wave conditions were calm at two to three feet high and the boat handled smoothly at twenty-two to twenty-five knots, Boss's usual cruising speed.

The two girls, bikini clad, blonde and shapely, graced the forward deck as if posing for some Playboy poster. As soon as they were a few miles from shore, the girls peeled off their tops and rubbed each other down with suntan oil. They lay back down on the nice cushions to gladly display their many God-given gifts. Boss viewed the wonderful display of human flesh and could not help but think about a story he heard once. It was about an African preacher who asked one of his colleagues if it was wrong to take pleasure in the opposite sex, in his case, his organist. His colleague asked him if it was true that he had a wife who actually supported his family. The preacher answered "yes" to the question. "And is it true that you have minor children at home?"

The preacher again answered, "Yes."

"Well, friend, you know it's wrong to commit adultery and harm your wife and children," said the colleague.

"Yes," said the preacher, "but you agree that everything good comes from God, don't you?"

The preacher's colleague thought for a minute and agreed that all good things do come from God.

The preacher, who stuttered, replied, "Well, brother, she's so, so good that her sex has to be a good gift from God." The colleague looked puzzled at his friend and could not find the right response, so he just conceded to the preacher's point.

Boss gazed at the scenery on his forward deck and agreed these young ladies were a gift from God to be appreciated.

Boss cut on the radar and saw no traffic to worry about within the ten-mile radius. He put the range of protection at five miles ahead and engaged the autopilot. Victor already had a tray with drinks for everybody, so the two went forward to join the lovely ladies. As they walked toward the ladies, Boss repeated the story about the preacher to Victor and they both had a laugh as proponents of the preacher's view.

"Ah, ladies, what could be better than a beautiful day, a fine yacht, good company and pina coladas for everybody?" Boss asked with his most seductive voice.

The next hour was spent in laughter and general debauchery. Boss, having satisfied his lust for the female body, was, in the way of most men, ready to leave the ladies to their private moments when they chitchatted about things only a woman could comprehend. Boss was sure that they would be bitching about men taking care of their own needs but not satisfying the female needs. And of course, they would be complaining about how the men never talk to them or really understand a woman's need to be understood. What the hell, thought Boss. He had satisfied his needs and it was time to take care of business.

Victor sat in the pilot's chair. There was no need to take charge of the helm until they got to the pass in Biloxi. Visibility was excellent and the radar was clear of any immediate targets, so Victor left the alarm ring of protection on in the radar. Speed and bearing were fine, so the autopilot was left in its present heading. Boss locked the door into the pilothouse, so there would be no interruption to their business conversation. Boss connected his satellite phone to the speaker, engaged the scrambler and initiated a call to Boston.

"Greetings, gentlemen. Victor and I are here as ordered," announced Boss.

"Everybody is here on this end. Go ahead and give us your report, Boss," came the gravelly voice of Number One on the other end. "We have received and reviewed your monthly information. Follow the usual protocol regarding documentation. At this point, we do not need a review of the documentation. Money matters are in order, so go on to the other matters."

Boss replied, "As you know, the biggest change is the transition from Reed to George Currier and his team. I can report that George is a far better man than Reed was. George comprehends all aspects of the business, including the necessary firewalls. He's especially effective in his ability to handle the Mexicans. He's been able to convince the Mexicans to handle their disagreements in Mexico. It seems the two cartels have worked out their differences over territorial lines, at least in the upper Panhandle. George also has our dealers in line. They understand that it's far better for them to do business with us than to entertain the alternatives. Other elements of the business are under control. The loan business is good and the gold and mortgage businesses are good.

"Our real estate business is good. As you know, I'm able to buy up properties at very low prices. Many good income-producing properties are available for a steal. You need to review the summary I sent and you will see it would be wise to transfer most of these existing properties to other companies. It will free up funds to help us stay on top of all the good deals that come along."

Number One said, "Boss, you keep using that term 'good deal,' but you know these aren't good deals on the open market. They're only good deals to us because we have to keep the money working. When we have to go to the open market, many of these deals only make sense on the basis that it cleans up liquid assets. What I'm telling you is to make sure you don't over pay for any property and that you stick with property based on the value to income ratio."

"Of course you're right," said Boss. "We don't pay enough to look suspicious. We don't buy a property that looks distressed. We don't buy dark shopping centers unless we have a plan in place to revive it. While we're bottom feeders, what we have are good projects at bottom feeder prices."

When Boss completed his report, Victor gave his view of the off-line trade. The conversation then moved to the overall mood in the area due to the high murder and death rates and their impact on off-line businesses. Boss let them know there was an investigation trying to tie all these events together, but that at this point, their operations had yet to be connected to any of the murders. Boss concluded the businesses were as safe as they could make them and that they were cutting their exposure as much as was possible. He assured them that his team would keep an especially sharp eye on the situation, at least until things cooled off. The meeting went on for a little over an hour until headquarters in Boston was satisfied they had covered themselves as much as possible.

With the meeting over, Victor and Boss were ready for another round of partying. Boss brought the girls up to the pilothouse where the debauchery resumed. Boss grabbed his girl, slid her bikini off, sat her in the captain's chair and then entered that place where he didn't care where the yacht was headed.

Meanwhile, in a plush office in downtown Boston, three men sat around a large conference table sipping coffee. Number One spoke. "Gentlemen, seems like we have a little problem in the Panhandle. Too many killings, too much attention, too many eyes trying to locate our businesses. Sooner or later, the authorities will get a break and we may have to move quickly."

"I agree," said Number Two, the man to the right of the head chair. "Boss has done an excellent job and is one of our top producers. Hopefully events will not overtake him."

Number Three, the man to the left of the head chair, inquired about their ability to replace Boss if necessary. To this, Number One responded, "We can move our man out of Atlanta or we can simply move the main office out of Pensacola to Atlanta. The drug and gold business we could leave in the Panhandle. The funny mortgage business is a localized kind of operation, which we can't leave in any one location for very long. We can easily replace that operation in a new area. We always move that operation to new areas every four to five years. Any longer presents too many risks. I don't want to retire Boss unless it becomes absolutely necessary. We give Boss whatever help he needs and at the same time have our secret watchers keep a close eye on him and make sure we're kept fully informed."

The group in Boston completed their meeting, accepted their various assignments and adjourned to dine on a great steak at their favorite restaurant.

Hard work created a large appetite in these big boys. The spirited discussion of life and death matters always left them in a lighthearted, giddy mood. These men had removed themselves from the blood and guts of their business. The dark side of their business was in one way a distant memory. They were respected businessmen; at least that's what they saw when they looked in the mirror.

By the time Boss, Victor and the girls docked the yacht, went to the casino and returned to the yacht, the eastern sky was just beginning to show evidence of the rising sun. The girls retreated to their rooms, but Boss took Victor aside into the main lounge. "Victor," said Boss, "before it slips my mind, I need to warn you not to have any contact with Suzy. I'm aware of your tendency to obsess over certain kinds of women and I suspect that you have a little bird in your head singing a siren's song about the lovely Suzy. This may be your only weakness, Victor. Do not make that mistake. The girl has received special training and she's capable of taking care of herself. If you contact her, the odds are high that she'll end up on somebody's watch list."

"Okay, Boss." Victor smiled. "I understand. I'll keep my dick in my pants. I won't go anywhere near the woman. But you don't really think that little girl could hurt me, do you? Damn, Boss, I thought you were more impressed with me than that."

"Yeah, you're a tough guy, Victor, but this girl is being watched. You get close to her, they'll find out who you are and then shit will hit the fan. You know as well as I do that the boys in Boston will not put up with that kind of mistake. Now, promise me you'll stay away from her."

"Sure thing, Boss. I promise. I wouldn't touch her with yours, much less mine," replied Victor.

The men separated and went to their births tired but satisfied that they had pulled from life all it had to offer for that day. The world, for that moment, was under control.

— 16 —

Seven a.m. sharp, Chic, Heath, Ken and Bob Funk met at the clubhouse at Kelly Plantation in Destin, Florida.

"The history of the Kelly property golf course is worthy of a book," said Chic, who was a student of local history.

"Okay, Chic," said Heath, "we've got thirty minutes until tee time. You think you can tell the story that fast?"

"Go ahead," said Bob. "Lay it on us."

"Well, it goes back to the late thirties and forties when the land wasn't worth anything. There wasn't even a bridge from the mainland over to the barrier islands. All the sandbar was good for was to stop the big waves from hitting the mainland. A lot of the land was owned by Eglin Air Force Base. This land wouldn't grow anything, not even a good pine tree. The pine trees were stunted and were only good for production of turpentine. At that time, you could buy this beach for twenty-five to fifty cents an acre. You were lucky if you could produce enough income to pay your property taxes.

"The fishing was great. Mr. Kelly made enough money from commercial fishing and used his profits to buy a bunch of this worthless sand on the Barrier Islands. In fact, he owned several miles of beachfront property. As time went by, this worthless sand became very valuable. As roads and bridges connected the mainland to the islands, sports fishermen began to come to Destin by the droves.

"The story goes that some of the fisherman created the present Destin Pass by digging a ditch, which the hurricane washed out, creating the pass."

Ken chimed in, "Well, I'm glad I know who's to blame for that terrible pass. Of all the passes I've been through, Destin Pass has to be the worst ever. In the wrong wind and tide conditions, you can bottom out very quickly. They've actually lost a coast guard boat in that pass."

"Yeah," said Heath. "Don't try it with a north wind and an incoming tide."

"For all I know," said Chic, "old Kelly might have been the guy actually responsible for that pass. Old Kelly lived into the sixties, had several kids and lost his wife of many years. As a true sailor and fisherman, Kelly promptly married a young fox. So he had two families when he died without a will. Naturally, the two sides of the family got into litigations that tied up several miles of valuable waterfront property for years.

"I think the story reaches its climax on a beautiful clear day like today. The new Mrs. Kelly and her friends and advisors were all out to sea when their boat exploded, killing all who were aboard. No one was able to prove why the boat exploded, but the beneficiary of this misadventure was the original family. It was not until recent years that the Kelly property became available for sale. That's the specific point when the Destin area went from a sleepy, little fishing village to the tourist mess of today."

"Well," said Bob, "looks like a story where good and right prevails over evil."

"Could be," said Chic, "but it might be a story illustrating that the love of money is the source of all evil."

"Now, boys, y'all are missing the point," said Heath. "As a law man, I can tell you that most killing involves pussy, hound dogs or property lines. Here we got two of the three: pussy and property. Do you think the new wife had a hound dog?"

"I think it certainly proves that an estate with a lot of money will bring out the worse in people," said Chic. "I took a pre-law course in college and the professor turned red in the face every time he got on the issue of administration of estates. You spend your life trying to accumulate assets, which in the later life can become a burden. Then you die and the family you're trying to help becomes bitter enemies, fighting over the assets you left.

"So much for philosophical bullshit. All it proves is that shit hits the fan. Let's hit the golf course so Ken and I can get some of your money."

It was a close match. All of them carried handicaps from eight to ten. Chic, when he was on, would beat anyone with his putting and today was his day. After settling the bets, Ken and Bob headed off to Ken's house on the bay and Heath and Chic dropped in at the Land & Sea for a reasonably priced seafood meal. Land & Sea was one of those small places run by Thais, whose food was always top notch. Heath and Chic sat outside, immediately adjacent to the traffic of US Highway 98. There was enough traffic noise to assure that Chic and Heath had a private conversation in this public place.

"How's the investigation going?" inquired Chic.

"As you might expect," Heath said, "Thomas Reed's safe must have contained his paperwork that we need to tie these criminal endeavors together. As you suggested, the ninjas were after the money and the other group was after the records. I've assigned one of my best detectives to the case. One is all I could talk the sheriff into sparing. We don't really have anything tying all the events of late together. We know we have a lot of drug related activity going on, but we haven't been able to relate the drug activities to Reed or the loss of his safe."

"I agree with you," Chic said as he scratched his chin in his best pensive frown. "What we have is a gut feeling that the killings of late, including the Reed deaths and Gertrude Wade's death, are all drug related. I also believe that we're dealing with money laundering. I haven't seen any clues that would direct me to a mafia connection. For example, we haven't seen any connection with prostitution, nor have we seen any Italian-looking guys around. The mafia leaves a certain type of trail, which is absent here. Of course, in today's world, crimes like this are more a product of a large syndication of people who may not look like or even be Italian. We have the Russians and other Eastern European people who are involved in this type of activity.

"What we do see is evidence of Mexican drug cartel activity, but nothing indicating that this is a fight between them and the mafia. It looks like a Mexican dispute over territory.

"I think if we're actually dealing with a criminal enterprise, they're highly organized, sophisticated and more akin to a regular business venture than a normal mafia operation. I also cannot identify anything that would make me believe this is related to the Eastern European type of syndicate."

Heath picked up on Chic's train of thought. "Hold that thought, Chic. The waiter is coming to take our order. What do you get here?"

"I always get the whole snapper. When they see me coming they check their inventory because they know that's what I order. If they don't have it, then they go get it from the fish market next door."

"Sounds good to me," replied Heath. "I'll get the same thing."

The waiter recognized Chic and after his usual greeting let Chic know they had whole snapper in stock. The waiter was a really nice guy who had emigrated here from Romania. Heath listened as Chic inquired about the waiter's progress at the local community college. As soon as they waiter left, Heath and Chic picked up their conversation.

"Chic, the problem is that we've had a hell of a lot of killing going on. Some of these have been professional hit jobs. The Mexican who was shot at the traffic light is an example.

"Then we have the two guys who disappeared from their car lot in Fort Walton a few days ago. We know of three more. We know where they lived. We know these families. We know they've been involved with drugs on a small scale in the past. We can't prove they're big distributors in this area. We know two were abducted from their car after work. We've established that sleeping gas was used to disable them. That's all we know, except that they've disappeared from the face of the earth.

"I agree that if these crimes were connected and we assume it's not the mafia, then we have a big problem. With the mafia, we would have a better feel for their operation. The FBI would at least have some broad connection that we could explore.

"It doesn't have the smell of Eastern European involvement. In our case, we seem to have an enterprise that's trying to keep a clean face. There may even be legitimate facets to their operations."

"Yeah, I think there's a legitimate side to their operation," said Chic. "That has to be the reason for the importance of Reed's safe to somebody. The detective you have working the case found records of financial transactions between several loan companies and some of Reed's customers. Seems like some guy named George is now calling on some of Reed's clients. Have we seen anything that would lead us to believe George is dirty?"

"Not at all," said Heath. "As you might expect, some of these car lots have been associated with drug activity in the past, but there's no indicator that George is involved. He has no criminal record. If we had a full investigation by the FBI or DEA issuing subpoenas, we might get a lead somewhere. The car lot and pawnshops owned by Reed haven't been taken over by George. We've seen no evidence that George ever does business with Reed's properties.

"We just don't have any information that would allow us to issue subpoenas. Reed's activities were investigated and nothing of interest was discovered. We did get the names of some of his clients, but these activities have been a matter of record and are apparently legal. Whatever illegal activity there was isn't a matter of record. Even his financial records don't disclose a large flow of cash."

"Every tentacle of the octopus leads to the head of the beast," said Chic. "We just have to find one tentacle that lives and the beast is ours. I think we're close. All these deaths mean that the beast has shed sacrificial parts of his body before we could get to the living connections. That means that the part of the beast that is shed must grow a new member. It's in the activity of growing this new part that we may find our break.

"We know that George has replaced Reed, at least in the legal part of his enterprise. Let's crosscheck the lending institutions that financed Reed with those now run by George. See if there's any connection."

"I'll get right on that, Chic. I'll give you a call when we have a chance to check that out. This will at least give us commonality to explore."

"Well," said Chic, "here comes our fish."

"Man, that looks good," said Heath. "Been a while since I've had whole snapper broiled like this."

Chic and Heath refilled their wine glasses with Pino Grigio and ate their whole red snapper. They parted with full bellies and clear minds.

Meanwhile, Ken and Bob made their way to Destin Harbor where Ken kept his fifty-foot Amel named *Amadee*. Ken suspected the Amel sailboat was the only good thing to come out of France. The crew kept the boat in excellent shape. All the sails were hydraulically controlled and Ken was capable of handling the boat by himself.

Two girls were already on board. They made sure provisions were on board for the weekend. As soon as Ken and Bob were aboard, the girls took in the dock lines and Ken made way to Destin Pass. Within forty-five minutes, they had cleared Destin Pass. They took a heading east to Panama City and engaged the autopilot. The festivities began. Ken always made sure on these events to have girls who loved sailing as much as he did. Nothing worse than a weekend sailing trip with women who got seasick or who rebelled against the close quarters of sailboat living.

Bob and Ken entertained the girls with tall tales about the guys at Fish House card games, which eventually lead to Ken's favorite game of strip poker. Nothing better, he thought, than the beautiful naked bodies of these two lovely women and so Ken's weekend of sailboat and debauchery began.

In these moments of true Hellenistic pleasure, Bob would come with his shot at comedy: "I wonder what the poor folks are doing right now. Reminds me of what the queen asked the prince on their wedding night. 'Sir Charles, is this what the common folks call fucking?' 'Why yes, my dear. Why do you ask?' 'Well, I want you to decree that they shall not do it. It is too good for them.'"

And so went the weekend.

— 17 —

Chic had recently missed several card games with the Fish House gang. He had been too busy with his work, his singing and, of course, teaching Suzy how to defend herself. He had grown fond of this little hell-fire and began to wonder who was teaching whom what. By now, he was convinced she could take care of herself, but he had to admit that he was developing a personal need to protect Suzy. He wasn't sure he truly understood the particular emotion he felt toward her. *All in good time*, he thought. *It wasn't easy to fight his animal instincts to simply take this girl. Not take, but to avoid being taken in by this little she-devil.*

Chic began to hum the tenor part of the love duet in act five of *Faust* by Charles Gounod. Chic loved *Faust* and had the opportunity to sing portions of *Faust* in Birmingham, Alabama, that summer. Perhaps he could deliver Suzy from her fate. He had taken Suzy to the last performance and set her up near the front where he could keep an eye on her. Probably not a good idea. He almost forgot a line when he held her gaze for a moment too long.

Chic couldn't help but laugh at himself for letting a girl disrupt his singing performance. He remembered the first time that happened. When just a freelancer, he was asked by his religion professor to lead the singing at a church where the professor was conducting a revival. It was a country church with a lot of pretty, young ladies around. There was an especially good-looking young lady with a small baby in the front row. In the middle of Chic's solo, the young woman unbuttoned her blouse, took out a marvelous breast and began to feed the young child. Chic remembered he had to do a "watermelon, watermelon" for a full verse before he could regain his composure. Chic was sure Mephistopheles had gotten a hold of him that night.

As Chic pulled his Mustang convertible up to Ken's house, his mind switched gears to the plotting necessary to win at cards tonight. While it was only penny ante poker, his motivation to win couldn't have been greater if they were playing for millions.

Chic couldn't help but be impressed by the number of big-boy toys Ken had. He had to be in the big time to afford this house, his boats, his office in Pensacola and the other trappings of wealth he displayed. Ken was an educated man and reflected well on his alma mater, Vanderbilt.

Chic didn't envy Ken. Chic's view of life wasn't necessarily motivated by wealth and power. A man had to be driven to sit where Ken now sat. He had power, money, women, boats and all the things most men crave.

Chic could certainly question his own choices in life. He knew he was not driven to pursue wealth with breakneck speed. Was he a hippy, a nerd or what? Tonight, for example, he knew he would take a little ribbing about having on his lace breeches because of his recent performance of *Faust*. He had developed a plan for that event. Chic had made the choices he liked. He had no drive to sacrifice himself to be a rich man. Chic knew the real price that Ken paid and that many other rich men paid to obtain their wealth.

And wealth, he knew, was not in and of itself wrong. In fact, in the hands of the master, a successful business was a work of art. Providing good jobs where people could make an honest living was as much a part of God's plan for man as was the formation of sea, air and land. Chic knew that his choices in life would not make him wealthy. His choices, however, made him happy.

Chic always remembered that old sailor and his wife he met at Isla Mujeres on one of his events where he worked on a yacht that was in the Pensacola-Cancun race. Chic was giving the old sailor some of his paperback books to read. He had found out that this old man and wife were retired teachers who lived in Florida. They got tired of waiting to die. In the retirement community, the daily activity was discussing who died that day and who might be next. They decided to go down with their boots on. They sold their house and worldly possessions, bought a twenty-five foot sailboat and headed south.

Their family was concerned about pirates and storms, but the old couple could only see adventure. So a storm gets them. So what?

As Chic gave the old sailor the books, the sailor looked at Chic and said, "You know, I've got everything a rich man has."

Chic, taking the bait, said, "How do you figure that?"

"Well," continued the old sailor, "how many beds can you sleep in at a time?"

"Only one," said Chic.

"I've got a bed, just like the rich man. How many clothes do you need?" asked the old sailor.

"I guess you can't wear but one set at a time," said Chic.

"I've got enough clothes. How much food can you eat?" asked the old sailor.

"Well, if you get right down to it, you can certainly live off a lot less than we actually eat," replied Chic.

"I have all the food I need and if I run out, I drop a line in the water and catch a fish. Now how many toothbrushes do you need at one time?" asked the old sailor.

"Only one," said Chic.

"I've got a toothbrush," said the old sailor. "How many houses do you need?"

"Only one at a time," replied Chic. "While you may have many, you only need one."

"My boat is my home and it's all I need. So I have everything a rich man has. I have a house. I have a bed. I have clothes. I have a toothbrush. I have all the food I need just like a rich man. But I have one thing a rich man doesn't have."

"And what would that be, Mr. Sailor?" asked Chic.

"Well, I'm happy. When is the last time you met a happy rich man?" inquired the old sailor.

"You got me there," said Chic. "I can't name one right off."

Since that time, Chic had been searching for a happy rich man. Chic, being the practical hardheaded observer that he was, took the large view of life. He believed the words of Christ when he spoke of the way being narrow and that few would find and follow the path of enlightenment. So, finding a truly happy person, rich or poor, was a real challenge.

Chic recalled the history professor who explained that there are three things that are common to all societies, large or small, urban or rural, developed or undeveloped. Those three things are religion, prostitution and a drug that affects the central nervous system. Chic recognized the truth of the professor's words. What intrigued Chic was the fact that each of these things was a form of escapism or was a reaction to the perceived difficulties of daily life. No man has escaped death or the tribulation of human existence. As a student of human nature, Chic knew that all humans struggled with life. In the end, the physical, material world prevailed over the body as a life form. Only in that metaphysical world of the spirit, which was not confined by physical dimensions of life, could man prevail over the physical world.

As Chic exited his Mustang and headed toward Ken's front entrance, he hoped no one brought up religion and philosophy tonight. Being in one of his contemplative moods, they'd probably throw him out of the game for talking too much philosophical bullshit. Bob would be on his butt for sure. Perhaps even worse, the conundrum presented by wealth vis-à-vis God's will couldn't be resolved by him. In the Jewish tradition, wealth was translated a blessing from God and poverty was looked upon as a curse from God. Christ revolutionized this belief by demonstrating that wealth could be an obstacle in the relationship between God and man. So Chic saw no need to confuse others with his own conflicted opinion on the subject.

"Good evening, men," said Chic. "Now that I'm here, the party can begin." Chic noticed that Ken had a couple of new girls tempting the men tonight. *This ought to be an easy night with all the guys looking at the pretty girls' asses instead of having their minds on the game.*

Syd was the first one to jump on Chic with the usual jab. "Chic, I know you've been associating with those tweety birds at the opera, so come over here and let me see if you got your lace breeches on."

Chic had actually attached some lace around the top of his boxer shorts, waiting for this opportunity. Chic compliantly walked over to Syd, who straightaway pulled down Chic's pants enough to expose what appeared to be laced breeches.

"Well, I see you finally came out of the closet," said Syd.

"You know, Judge," said Chic, "Suzy made this lace for me and I'd go dance in a tutu at the Met if the little beauty queen asked me to. If Suzy thinks I'm man enough for her, who can argue with that?"

Bob followed the repartee with, "Hell, if Suzy thinks old Lace Breeches here is man enough for her, then who am I to argue with her?"

"Hell, at least he didn't wear a pair of Suzy's panties," remarked Ken.

"Guys, I've never admitted this to anyone, but I guess I can confess all to you fellows. I know you wouldn't repeat this."

"You can bet your ass on that," said Ralph. "Unless it's like that joke I tell about the guy who, after a night of debauchery, confessed to having sex with a goat. If it's like that, then I might not remain silent."

"It's not that bad, Ralph," said Chic. "You know I used to usher at the opera performance in Atlanta and occasionally I would handle props for a dollar. Got a good view of backstage that way. I've always had these big, strong legs that look like a dancer's legs. Now don't get too excited there, Ken. So I went backstage to get a prop and this guy started feeling my thigh. In broken English, he directed me to a guy with a tutu, who told me to put it on. I was assigned the duty of replacing a sick dancer and given instructions to follow this other dancer. He had the pitcher and I had the chalice. I was given instruction and away I went, prancing on stage just like the professional dancer in front of me. I stood on stage for a few minutes, waiting on the big tenor to take the chalice, which he did, but not on cue. I then pranced off stage like I knew what I was doing. I made two dollars that night."

"Damn it all, Chic," said Percy. "Now you'll never be able to run for president. Too bad."

Syd laughed, flipped the elastic in Chic's shorts and called all hands to straighten up and play cards.

As the card game progressed, Bob opened up the subject of the ninja murders. "Judge, are you handling that ninja case?"

"No. Thank God for that," said Syd. The DA is going after the death penalty of course and based on what I know, he'll get it in most cases. It's not often you have the full case covered in HD living color.

"There are a lot of rumors going around, mainly spread by Randall Moss. He claims he was a hired killer, actually bragging about it. It doesn't really matter if he was hired or not, because he's guilty of coldblooded murder. There are all kinds of rumors about drugs, money laundering, Mexican cartels, but as far as I know, there's no hard proof tying any of this to Reed's murder. There have been a lot of crooks killing each other, but thankfully, they're killing each other and not the general public. What do you think about all this killing, Chic?"

"Judge, in a way, we could take the long view that no matter how hard we try, sadly the battle between good and evil is with us always. That battle will not be resolved until the end time. Judge, you and I have devoted our lives to putting the evil people behind bars. Have we actually made any headway?" asked Chic.

"Even if we could somehow solve the drug problem, we would still have evil among us, although we would have a lot less people in jail," Chic continued. "What we're seeing here in Fort Walton and the Panhandle is basically drug related. Drug traffic creates a large amount of cash, which has to be transformed into clean, untraceable money. The love of money is the root of all evil. Drugs will move a person to kill family, friends and anyone close at hand with money or anything of value to steal. The two together create fertile ground for evil's growth. What can we say, Syd? The worse thing a preacher, judge or police officer can do is to get sucked up in the illusion that they can somehow reduce the amount of evil in this world."

"I guess you're right," replied Syd. "Ken, what do you think leads people into criminal enterprises? One brother becomes a crook, the other a respected businessman and civic leader. Same parents. Same education. In fact, I've seen children raised in the worst of circumstances and who have no excuse for finding a way of succeeding in life, yet some of these very people become our greatest leaders. What goes on in the mind that would lead similar individuals into paths that differ so remarkably? As I look at the varmints who come before me, it becomes real easy to lose faith in human nature. This is the way God created the world. Every man has the possibility of doing good or doing evil and the same opportunities of turning to the dark side. Why?"

"Damn, Judge, why don't you ask me an easy question? To answer that question requires far more wisdom than I've got," said Ken. "I can't talk religion and philosophy like you and Chic, but I think it's basically simple. People just grow up, making choices along the way. They get opportunities along the way and those opportunities lead them in one direction or the other. No two people are confronted with the same set of opportunities. People are really not smart enough to see the long-range consequences of their actions. Some get sucked up in drugs and before long, the drugs control their life. Even if they can see they're headed in the wrong direction, if there's money involved, many are likely to go for the money. Money means security to people and history shows that many will sell their souls for security."

Bob, who had no particular interest in the struggle between good and evil, interjected his comments. "Well, we can conclude then that if we do wrong, it's okay because the devil made us do it. Now deal the cards. I need to get some money off you guys."

— 18 —

Victor was still dealing with his obsession with Suzy. If he personally took out Suzy, Boss or Boston would feed him to the fish. He had to maintain firewalls. He had to consider that George was a danger to him personally. Victor had no illusion about the ability of George to replace him in this operation. Should he contact George to do the job, George would immediately turn Victor in to either Boss or Boston. He knew they would eliminate him before he could touch Suzy. He had his hit men and his drug organization he could call on. He couldn't use the drug organization. They could deal out the drugs in a way that provided him a fairly good firewall, but violence for them was in the Mexican mode. No finesse. No good.

Sam, the tall hit man, would have to handle this job. Tall Sam had a personal score to settle with Suzy. She had been able to escape him at Gertrude's house. Unfinished business, so to speak. Tall Sam didn't like unfinished business. His level of thinking didn't go much beyond thinking of better ways to kill. Sam would not understand Boss's position on avoiding Suzy. In fact, Sam had a fantasy about killing Suzy and Victor had not bothered to explain Boss's position on the matter. Victor concluded that Sam was expendable. Whether he managed to kill Suzy or not, it was time for him to go. Sam had been Victor's go between far too long and he knew too much. Victor had used Sam for all the assassinations and for everyday contact with the drug dealers.

Weighing this problem required Victor to do the calculus of whether it was more beneficial to kill Sam or not. Victor had the benefit of consistency. Once he considered this kind of question, he always came down on the side of elimination. *Dead bodies tell no tales*, he thought. Victor, of course, understood that dead bodies do tell tales but not verbally. If properly disposed of, the only tale they would tell was their absence. Disposal of the body in this case might not be possible. Not a perfect setup but workable. Victor would closely monitor the situation and would take out Sam on the way back to his pad in Crestview.

Victor called Sam and they met at their usual rest stop on Interstate 10. Seated at a table in the park area, Victor went over the plans.

"Sam," said Victor, "this has to be strictly between the two of us. There's no reason for anyone else to know. Don't tell any of your buddies about his. They can't know the mark, the time or place. The police have an eye on this girl and if they get any info, before or after, you're toast. Understand?"

"Yeah, yeah, Victor. That little bitch won't get away from me again," said Sam.

Victor continued, "You'll have to case this girl for a few days to make sure that when you do this, she'll be alone. She's been in training, so don't get too headstrong. Assume she's capable of defending herself. Assume she can pick up a tail, so stay back. Don't get too close. I've briefed you on where she teaches, the hours of her classes, the days she normally sees Chic, where she lives and other details we've accumulated. We want this to look like a regular home invasion. Use your knife, not the gun. Rape her—but be sure to use protection. Don't leave any semen around. Mutilate her body so there are clear sexual overtones to this job. I don't think I have to tell you, but make damn sure you don't have a billfold, a cell phone or any other thing on you that can identify you. This has got to be clean. Finally, I've got to know the time and date so I can give you cover if necessary. You won't see me, but I'll have your back."

"Okay," said Sam. "Two weeks and I'll be ready. I'll give you the information on the details within ten days."

Victor reminded Sam that they would use their usual methods of contacting each other. Victor stayed at the table awhile longer after Sam left, enjoying all the young girls running around and the way many were walking their stupid little dogs. *What a waste of time. These women loved their dogs better than their husbands. How stupid was that?*

Victor couldn't help but feel a little smug with himself. He worked with a smart group of people. Everything was done on a business-like basis. Didn't have any wild cowboys acting crazy and looking like dumb, uneducated, common criminals. This crowd had never been truly penetrated by the cops. He was actually proud of his astute decision with Sam. It's important to know when to close a possible source of information. With Sam gone, there would be no way to tie him to the recent killings. There would be no way of tying him to killing Suzy. His ability to make these difficult decisions was exactly why he had progressed in their organization. His ability to manage separated him from Sam and the worker bees in the drug trade and made him king of the hill.

Sam chose a Wednesday night. Chic usually had some church activity on that night and Suzy usually got home a little late. Lights were normally out by eleven p.m. His plan was to attack her right as she cut off the table lamp. This would give him the element of surprise. He planned on securing her hands and feet to the bed and then raping her. Sam didn't like having sex with dead bodies, although he understood a lot of morticians were into this kind of kinky sex. He figured he would have to knock her out first, which didn't seem to present a real problem. She wasn't, after all, a very big girl.

Sam took his full-size k-bar to do the job. When he arrived, he secluded himself in the bushes outside the living room window. Suzy didn't get home until after dark, so Sam had plenty of time to prepare the window for easy opening. He knew he could enter this window with no noise and without disturbing any furniture. Sam waited until Suzy was bathing and then entered the house and positioned himself under the bed. Sam had planned well. He got a wonderful view of Suzy as she walked from the bathroom naked. Sam's anticipation built to the point he could hardly control his animal instincts to devour this sexual goddess. Suzy slipped into a very small nighty, got her book and hopped into bed. She read for about thirty minutes, which seemed like hours to Sam.

Control yourself, Sam thought. *Why don't I just pop up and slit her throat, get some pussy and get out of here?* No, he didn't want to make that kind of mess. Stick to the plan. He heard Suzy close the book and lean over to her right to turn off the lamp.

As Suzy rolled back to her left, Sam, who was under the bed on the left side, slid from under her bed and lunged for her neck, attempting to get her into a chokehold. As luck would have it, Suzy was moving forward to pull up the cover at the same moment Sam's head was coming forward. The top of Suzy's head hit Sam square in the nose, instantly breaking it. Fortunately for Suzy, the top of her head was a lot harder than Sam's nose. The impact stunned Sam and frightened the hell out of Suzy.

Suzy proved to be a cool customer under pressure. Chic's training had drilled into her reflexes, which saved her life. With her cat-like reflexes, she pushed to her right, grabbed the pink .38 caliber pistol with her right hand and with one smooth motion held Sam off with her left hand. She jammed the pistol into Sam's chest and fired three shots. Sam rolled to his left, fell off the bed and was dead by the time he hit the floor.

Suzy was thankful that Chic made her learn all her defensive moves from both the left and the right. She never really believed that she would actually have to shoot another human being. It took a moment for the reality of the situation to impress itself on Suzy's conscious mind. She found herself standing above the intruder with the gun pointed at his head. Had she killed the attacker? There was enough ambient light in the room for her to at least vaguely make out the body on the floor. Without thinking, the pistol seemed to explode with its own volition into the head of the prone body. Suzy circled to other side of the bed and turned on the bedside lamp.

Suzy maintained her defensive posture. Looking at the bloody man on the floor, she relaxed for a second or two until the realization struck her that if this was one of the killers involved in Gertrude's murder, there may be another lurking in her house. *Where was the other guy?* Now she had to face the dilemma of taking time to dial 911 or first make sure there was not a second killer in her house. Suzy took a quick inventory of her bedroom and decided to lock her bedroom door and then dial 911.

Victor had secluded himself close enough to the house to hear the first muffled shots and later a louder shot. Victor knew at this point that Sam brought a knife to a gunfight and had lost the argument. It was possible Sam used Suzy's gun, but in his gut, he knew better.

Victor's first impulse was to go into the house and finish the job. If Suzy had the gun, his odds of pulling off a clean job were nil. His only real choice was to wait and see if Sam came out or if the police and ambulance showed up first.

Before Victor had time to actually move toward the house, he heard the sirens in the distance. The shots paced out as they were told Victor that this little redheaded vixen had the makings of a coldblooded killer. She had actually executed the coup de grace. Sam was dead. One problem solved.

Victor had parked his car in a place where he could easily leave without confronting any police or ambulance approaching the scene. As Victor drove back toward his house, he had to struggle with his desire to reward the girl or to kill her ... or, better yet, obsess over what a hell of a partner in crime she would make. *How could one little redhead cause him this much trouble?*

Victor, being the professional he was, quickly directed his thinking about how to report this to Boss. He had already concluded that if Sam were killed, it would save him the trouble. He had hoped Suzy would be killed in the process, but it was not to be. Victor, at that moment, erased Suzy from his mind.

He would simply wait for the local news sources to report the killing and then he would call Boss. Victor would, of course, be as surprised as Boss about the event, but Boss would be pleased that Sam had been eliminated. Boss would conclude that Sam was no longer a threat to them.

The next morning on the seven a.m. news, Suzy dominated the new reports. Looking great, even in charge of the interview, the entire story was revealed in great detail. The police reported there was no identification on the body and there was not enough face left to identify by photograph. Fingerprints and dental records would have to be used. The news did disclose that the dead body was a male Caucasian, brown hair, six feet two inches tall and weighing approximately one hundred eighty pounds. There was a dragon tattoo on his back, which was shown on the news. No other identifying marks could be found on the body.

Boss was watching the morning news on his yacht in Pensacola. Boss immediately knew this had to be Tall Sam, which was confirmed by the dragon tattoo. Before Boss could call Victor, his scrambled hand phone rang. It was Victor. They agreed to meet at their usual fishing hole, Victor in his fishing boat and Boss in his small fishing boat.

It was a good day for fishing. Victor had already reeled in a couple of red fish before Boss arrived. Anchor dropped, both boats side by side, the meeting began. There was no time for small talk today.

Boss began, looking Victor in the eyes, "Okay, Victor, tell me you didn't have anything to do with Sam trying to kill Suzy."

"No, sir, Boss. I'm not that crazy," replied Victor. "I called you as soon as I saw it on the news. Until they showed that tattoo on Sam's back, I didn't believe it had anything to do with our people. To my knowledge, Sam has never been to prison, so they might not have any fingerprints on him. I assume, however, that they'll eventually be able to identify him. I really don't see any way they can trace him to us. He was our only contact with other people who worked with him. He's dead, so he can't identify us as being related to any other activity. In fact, they'll never be able to identify him as one of the killers in Gertrude's case. I think this looks like what it probably is. Some crook seeing this pretty girl on TV and deciding to act on his passions. This was on his own dime, Boss, not ours."

"I think I believe you on that," said Boss. "As much as you wanted that redheaded bitch, I don't think you would want to share her with another pussy hound. I think we can all accept now that she's dangerous and we must stay clear. Even though the police can't tie Sam to any other jobs involving us, it still keeps the spotlight on the entire situation. We don't need any spotlights on our type of activity. You never know where they might get a break and then we're in trouble. Make sure that all our people are keeping their heads down. Don't take any stupid chances. Tell George to keep a close eye on the lawyer, Albert Barnes. He could be a loose cannon, so reel his operations in for a while."

Victor agreed that they had to keep a tight rein on Barnes. "Boss, I'll get the word around. We'll pull operations in close to the vest for a while."

The two men brought in their rods and reels and went their separate ways.

The news of Sam's death reached Boston by the nine a.m. breakfast meeting of the managing triad. The general feeling was that while this may not be a company project, Sam was still related to company activity. They didn't see any way this could complicate things, especially since Sam was dead. They all agreed his death was a good thing.

Number One brought up the obvious. "Do we need to reel in our exposure through Boss's operations?"

"Yes," replied Number Two.

"Number Three, give us the operational details of how we can do that and how fast," said the chair.

"As you know," said Number Three, "since Reed's death, we have already strengthened our firewalls. We've sent George in, who's capable of taking over any part of the operations in Florida if necessary. We're in the process of selling all of our legal properties in the open market and we should have this completed within the next thirty days. The management functions have been transferred to independent companies. Boss's operations can continue to fulfill the management duties on short-term contracts until the independent companies can get up to speed. The title loan companies, pawnshops and other loan operations have been assigned to offshore sources, which we do not believe can be traced back to us. This is part of our routine operation. The property mortgages on homes are never recorded and that cash is simply fed back into the system. Some used for gold purchases. We can change the source of the gold-operating funds on a weekly basis if we have to and we'll sell the gold to other sources.

"Now, in the process, we've actually created, along with the money from the cartel, a substantial source of available cash, which can't really be traced through Boss. So we have reduced our exposure there, which is actually good for Boss, as well as for our other operations. Boss can still originate a lot of loans and we will simply fund most of these by pre-selling the paper in the open market. Boss's companies will owe for bridge loans to our offshore private banks, so the money will flow as usual. Boss keeps five to six million in cash in his safe, which we'll deal with if necessary.

"So," continued Number Three, "if things go south, we might have to move Boss's operations, but basically it would be more of an inconvenience rather than a loss of a lot of money."

Number One joined in, "Some of our people may go, but the business remains intact, lost in the labyrinth of daisy chains and legitimate business transactions. That's good. Now make sure we don't lose control of any of the moving parts here. Boss is one of our best producers, so we'll save him if we can."

— 19 —

Suzy was a woman of the world, having lived life to its fullest. This is not to say that Suzy was proud of everything she had done. Even when she behaved like a common slut, she had to admit that it was exciting. Killing a man in her bedroom, however, was the bridge too far. *Is this what they meant when they talked about the fruit of sin being death?* Suzy had to face the truth about herself. That truth was that she never learned anything the easy way. *Was this the natural consequence of loose living, low morals and just generally acting like a bitch dog in heat? Was this any way to learn the lessons about the benefit of righteous living?*

She had heard that there was no person stronger at good moral living than a repented whore. Suzy rebelled at the very thought that she might be a whore. After a few moments of thinking about the subject, she had to admit that there wasn't any difference in a whore and a girl experimenting with sport sex with any half-good looking man in sight and even including a girl or two for additional pleasure. The fact she didn't charge for her service wouldn't save her from being branded as a whore.

As the night wore on, Suzy approached that place in her soul where she was ready to change her life. In between talking to police officers, detectives and news media, there was ample time to reflect on her life. Reflective thinking was new to Suzy. *Would this night never end?*

From the time the police arrived, it was constant pandemonium. Same questions, same statements, over and over. First at her home and then at the police station. The police looked at the knot on her head but otherwise were unconcerned with her condition.

Thank God she had called Chic right after she called 911. If Chic hadn't been there, she wouldn't have been able to handle the pressure.

The hardest part was when they accused her of murder. There was no reason to shoot this guy in the head, they said. He didn't have a gun and his knife had not been drawn. After some tall talking, Chic was able to get Suzy released into his custody, but not before five a.m.

The chief finally come into the interrogation room a little before five with his pronouncement. "Chic, we've decided to release Suzy into your custody for the time being, but you've got to have her back in here by three p.m. The DA is going to look at this and he'll decide if any charges will be filed against her. You know the routine. Since there's a death involved, it has to be presented to the grand jury. They'll have the last say in this."

"Okay, Chief," said Chic. "I think you know that Suzy is lucky to be alive. This perp didn't have tea for two in mind. The only reason he didn't reach his k-bar is because I trained Suzy well and that, combined with her athletic ability, was too much for this fiend. We've been expecting this assault and it came. Do what you can, Chief. This little lady has suffered enough."

"All right, Chic. I'll do what I can. Now take her home and have her back here at three p.m."

Suzy and Chic didn't say much walking to his Mustang. The adrenaline had worn off and only emptiness remained for Suzy. Chic, for his part, was concerned with identifying the perp. Chic didn't believe that this was a pervert trying to ravage and kill a good-looking woman he had seen on the news. The circumstances of her escape from Gertrude's house would certainly arouse the passions of more than one man. This guy, though, was far more careful than the pervert with rape and murder on his mind. This pervert had no identification on his person at all. He did have a rubber in his pocket, which told Chic that he had planned this very well.

Suzy had mentioned that the tall guy seemed to be in charge at Gertrude's house. While this guy was tall, Suzy couldn't identify him. Chic was curious about the absence of a gun. Chic was convinced that the knife was selected as a weapon instead of a gun to mislead the police from finding a pattern. There was also the practical consideration related to the identification of the perp's gun with other crimes. While one could argue that there was no real evidence here that would tie the perp to Gertrude's death or any of the other murders of late, Chic was willing to ride with his intuition that there was a connection.

Chic was a firm believer in the value of intuitive thinking. In many instances, he recognized the value of counter intuitive thinking. Either way, you needed to understand intuitive thinking in order to figure out how the solution often lay in the counter intuitive path. Chic never pressed his mind to form an epiphany, but where one appeared, he generally acted upon it.

Here, he developed a clear picture in his mind of the two perps involved in Gertrude's death and planning Suzy's death with masters behind the scene. His vision was that while there was an extensive criminal enterprise involved, the root of it all was money laundering.

Suzy represented a loose end that had to be taken care of. Chic would make certain that the chief devoted the necessary resources to identify the perp.

Someone would recognize the tattoo on the perp's back. There should be fingerprints on file. The perp had to get to Suzy's house either in his car or somebody had to drop him off. Most likely he was a loner, so there had to be a car parked somewhere in the neighborhood. The police had spent all night with Suzy and at the scene and he was sure there had to be a car somewhere close by. He couldn't leave Suzy alone in her condition, so on the way to his car, he called the chief on his cell phone. The chief was indisposed at the time, so as fate would have it he had to leave a message with one of the detectives. Chic knew that valuable time was being lost looking for clues in less productive areas.

As a professional criminal, Victor had developed a greater understanding of police procedures than had the average police officer. Victor knew where Sam had parked his car. It was in a car park several blocks from the scene of the crime where it would take several days to discover it was abandoned. Sam understood that in a solo operation in a neighborhood like this, you didn't want some neighbor identifying you by a car tag.

Victor knew he had at least a few hours before the police would canvass the area and they would not be waking the neighbors at two or three in the morning.

Victor called one of his recovery guys who handled all his repossessions. Sam's car was gone by two a.m.

Had the police found Sam's car, they would have been able to quickly identify Sam, find where he lived and search warrants would have been issued. God only knows what information they could have uncovered. The likelihood of hard evidence linking Sam to Victor was small, but even a note or some reference to Victor or his finance company would be bad. Victor's good fortune was a result of good planning; he had anticipated this problem. Since he had decided to whack Sam before he got to his car meant that disposal of his car was part of the overall plan.

As Chic was driving Suzy home, he felt like too much time had passed for them to find the car and this would be a lost lead. They should look, of course, but if this perp was part of the organization that killed Gertrude, they were too careful to leave this kind of loose end. The car, unless it was stolen, would have opened up this case. By the time the police canvassed the neighborhood, they were unable to get a lead on Sam's car. Chic still needed a break that would lead him to the organization.

On the other side of the equation, the fact that no car was found indicated the involvement of other people. This perp would not have used any method of transportation that could be easily traced. Since no car was found, that meant there was another individual involved in the attempted murder or other people were aware of the perp's death and had taken the precaution of removing the vehicle. On the positive side, the absence of a vehicle indicated the involvement of other criminal minds.

Except for Suzy killing the perp, the crooks were still ahead of them. There were a lot of dead people with no real evidence of any connection, except in Chic's mind.

Suzy laid the passenger seat back and went to sleep. Chic had seen enough of this little lady to know that she was as tough as nails, physically and mentally. She was able to control her emotions and slide her mind into neutral. Deep sleep came fast, notwithstanding the night's trauma. Suzy woke bright-eyed as Chic was pulling into his driveway, as though she had been trained for battle all her life.

"Chic," said Suzy, "let me sleep a few hours and I'll be ready to roll."

Chic got Suzy to the spare bedroom and then withdrew to his own space for what turned out to be a fitful five-hour nap. He finally got out of bed, went to the kitchen to make some coffee and was surprised to see Suzy seated at the table calmly sipping her coffee. She was wearing Chic's robe, which looked a lot better on her than on him.

"Suzy, you look right spry this fine morning. How do you manage that after the night you've had?"

"Easy," she said. "I decided that it's a whole lot better to be alive than dead. Nothing that's going to happen today is going to change that. I don't want to give you a big head, Chic, but I decided that it's pretty nice sitting here waiting on a good-looking guy like you to join me for a cup of coffee. More importantly, Chic, I've decided after careful thought that a life of debauchery was dangerous and not becoming of a good Southern girl like myself."

Chic blushed a little and tried to control himself as best a red-blooded American boy could. "Suzy, you know how to punch my buttons, that's for sure. But I don't have to tell you that. You know my weakness better than I do."

"In a way, I'm yanking your chain," she said. "If I truly trusted myself to not totally hurt you with my known bad habits, I would let you get a little closer to me. I understand that decent people like you can't share their woman with other men. It has finally dawned on me that it's time for me to change my ways. This is a pretty hard way to learn that there's a right way and a wrong way to live life. I haven't had much practice in the right way. Chic, you might have to help me with that. I promise not to tempt you anymore until I decide I'm serious about changing my life."

"Now, Suzy, you know I'm just human and subject to the same temptations as everyone else. I haven't put any pressure on you to change your life, although I have no doubt that only Christ can quench your thirst. There is no other path to having a full and satisfying life. What you've gone through has given you insight into what's important in life and what's not important. I don't have to tell you that you have a special place in my heart, but I've held back because I'm not that man who can control your passions. Only you can make those decisions and there's no way I will ever pressure you to change your life. I think way too much of you, Suzy, to jump in bed with you just to satisfy my own personal needs. As much as I think that would be wonderful, it would eventually turn both of us off and ruin whatever chance we would have at a solid relationship."

"I feel the same way," Suzy said. "As much as I desire you, I think I'm beginning to understand the value of a true relationship. God played a trick on us humans. He made sex so wonderfully exciting and then hedged the bet with a long list of negatives."

Suzy got up, laid a big kiss on Chic, sat down and with a determined look on her face, declared, "I guess it's going to be your job to finish raising me. I have a lot to learn to become a solid citizen. I believe I've had the devil scared out of me, so I'm ready to listen."

They agreed to meet for supper each night and Chic would give her Bible lessons from the gospels of Matthew, Mark, Luke and John.

By the time Chic returned Suzy to the chief's office at three p.m., the chief was looking at a different woman—a difference he couldn't quantify but a different persona nonetheless.

The DA and chief were waiting on them. The DA took charge. "Suzy, we've looked at this case carefully and we understand you acted in self-defense. How you managed to defeat this guy is a total mystery. I just have to assume you have a guardian angel watching over you. Any normal person would have been killed at Gertrude's house and no normal person would have escaped from this perp last night. If you didn't have that knot on your head and the blood splatter on your person and on the bed, we might have believed you didn't have to shoot him the second time. But the physical evidence is consistent with your story. We've determined that the guy was hiding under your bed. He probably broke into your house while you were in the shower.

"The perp was dead when you shot him in the head. That was a little too much, but we understand why you would have done that. Very few people would have had the presence of mind to take the last step.

"From our point of view, this is a self-defense case. It is our policy to present all violent death cases to the grand jury and they will have the final say. We expect them to agree with us in this matter.

"Chic, what's your opinion on the attempted murder?"

Chic reviewed his theory on the entire case, including his theory that this perp was part of the criminal conspiracy that had eluded him to this point. "It's my opinion," said Chic, "that we've seen the last of the attempts on Suzy's life. If my theory is correct, this group is well organized and will not attempt another shot at Suzy. The risk of exposure is too great. From their point of view, any overt act of violence creates a risk of exposure and they seem to appreciate the law of averages. I'd appreciate it if the chief would keep me posted on any information about the guy's identification, contacts, friends, computers, phones or anything else that would help me tie all these events together."

"We can do that," replied the chief. "I'll put Heath in charge. I know you two are working together on all of this."

"Thanks, Chief. Are Suzy and I free to go?"

"Sure." The chief actually cracked a smile and told them to get out of there. "Go enjoy the day and get your minds off this garbage."

Raw oysters at the oyster shanty, white sand, a slight breeze and the cooing sounds of two developing lovebirds blinded life's imperfections for Suzy and Chic.

— 20 —

Attorney Albert Barnes couldn't help but notice a slowdown in his loan closing since the death of Thomas Reed. The loans he did have were being moved around to surrounding counties, which took up more of his time. He made too much money on these loans to bitch, but he still wasn't happy with the slowdown. George kept him supplied with a small amount of drugs, but he needed more. Occasionally he supplied his girlfriend with drugs, but her supply was low. He had been able to fulfill the need through some transient guys, one of whom had a dragon tattoo on his back. He knew this guy as Tall Sam. Sam liked to show off his fancy tattoo, so he immediately recognized the dead man on TV. It took him awhile to remember the whole story about this Suzy girl escaping death at the site of a love triangle gone bad.

Why in the hell would Tall Sam try to kill this girl? Albert had no reason to connect all this to the outfit he was working for. All he really knew was that Reed and George helped him with the mortgage business and with his drugs. *What the hell?* He knew that Sam had a partner who sometimes filled in for him, so he wasn't worried that Sam's death was going to slow up his drug supply.

Unknown to Albert, his girlfriend, Marie, also had her own source of drugs, independent of Albert. Marie understood the need to have more than one source, just in case. Albert didn't have to know the details of how she paid for the drugs.

The DEA had Marie's supplier under surveillance, which led them to Marie. They then began to monitor Marie and this led them to Albert. There is nothing the DEA would rather do than nail a lawyer. Had they been more patient, they would have discovered Sam's buddy who sold drugs to both of them. They would have probably learned about Albert's mortgage business.

Had they been cooperative with the local authorities, this information would have filtered its way back to the chief and eventually to Chic.

Jumping too soon was a problem with some of the younger DEA boys. It's kind of like the story of the old bull and the young bull. The young bull wanted to run down the hill and screw one of the cows. The old bull told the young one, "Let's walk down the hill and screw them all."

When the young DEA officers knew they could nail a lawyer, they couldn't wait. They knew Marie had the drugs in the house with the lawyer, so they rushed in for an immediate arrest. Sure enough, they found not only Marie's drugs, but Albert also had a pretty good stash. These two looked like equal-opportunity drug users: cocaine, crack, marijuana and assorted pills. Not enough to qualify Albert as a big dealer, but they knew Albert would sing like a canary … and so he did, up to a point.

The DEA officers took them to separate rooms. Marie was more than willing to sing. Her problem was that the officers knew as much about her business as she did. She could only be useful to them as bait. She would have to be a stool pigeon. The young DEA guys warmed up to this idea. Marie was a good-looking honey and could be very useful as a protected dealer. She would be provided drugs for sale and all she had to do was turn in her customers. Occasionally they would use her to buy drugs from a dealer. She would be effective for a while. Sooner or later, she would be discovered and that would be it. They could only hope that she wouldn't be shot in the process. This was her problem, not theirs.

After a couple of hours, Marie agreed to the arrangement, although she was concerned about her safety. One of the more personable young officers hugged her neck and calmly assured her he would keep an eye on her at all times. He wouldn't let anything happen to her.

Marie thought about this for a few minutes. *How can I be sure?* She decided that she liked this young officer. She was confident that once she bedded him, he would be hers forever. He wasn't going to find anything like her around here. She understood the weakness of men and had no problem exploiting that with a little sexual experimentation. If anybody was going to be freaked out, it was not going to be her. She delighted in building up a man's ego. She was confident from experience that her honey trap was unbeatable. She pondered the stupidity of most women who tried to control men by rationing the gates of heaven when in fact the only way to gain power and control over men was happily giving access to womanly pleasure. Aphrodite was no fool. This young boy was hers. She could see clearly that she was to become an indispensable part of his team.

The young DEA agent didn't try to understand what was truly going on. He knew he had this young lady under his power. He was necessary for her to maintain freedom. He felt a wave of pleasure from some unknown source deep within his core. Somewhere in his brain, that primitive man recognized he had lost control. His conscious mind had developed way too many barriers to accept impulses from the primitive. Animal instincts were to be suppressed. Besides, he was quite confident that he and animals had nothing in common.

The "A" team worked on Albert. They used every trick in their book. Their main line was a promise to handle this off the record and not cause him to lose his law license if he would fully cooperate. He was open and honest about his drugs purchased from a drifter he claimed not to know. He claimed ignorance about Marie's supplies. So it went the first night in jail. It finally became apparent that they were getting nowhere useful with Albert. At this point, they only had a case of possession against Albert, which was not going to keep him in jail for long.

Albert was able to make the ten-thousand-dollar bond the next day and get out of jail. The DEA made it clear to Albert that the matter would be kept under wraps for a couple of weeks, but if he didn't come up with some solid information, he was in deep trouble.

Albert spent the next couple of days debating his situation. Marie had cut him off and wanted nothing else to do with him. *Damn fickle woman. She had gotten him in the middle of this mess and now it was his fault. What's going on with that woman?*

Albert knew he was on the horns of a dilemma. He couldn't get near drugs. He had handled enough drug cases to understand the program. They were just waiting for him to screw up. If he opened up about his mortgage business, he had no doubt that his life would be in jeopardy. If he didn't open up, he would go to jail and suffer the loss of his law license. His ability to make a living was in jeopardy because he couldn't handle any more loans. The DEA would be watching him for any unusual activity. Albert had no doubt they would uncover his illegal operation with George and eventually his connection to Reed.

What the hell was he going to do? Did he need to call George and tell him what was going on? What if his phone was tapped? Albert realized that he was in deep shit either way. He began to formulate a plan, but nothing he came up with was safe.

Albert began to wander around in a daze. No drugs. No pussy. Nowhere to turn. He finally retreated to Jack Daniels. For three days, he was in a drunken twilight. On the fourth day, he began to realize that he had to deal with this problem one way or another. *After all, how serious could this really be?*

Albert should have figured out that the people he worked for had ears everywhere. Had he realized this, he would have understood that his choices were far more limited than he thought.

Albert had no concept of the scope of the syndicate that made his little scheme possible. His little business washed around four to five million a year, which was chump change. It was convenient for George to use this money in pawn titles, pawnshops, bribes and general off-line activities. It was part of the money Boss kept in his vault. Even Albert knew this wasn't enough money to get anyone really excited. Compared to drug operations, it was small. He didn't see this as a drug related activity. The only thing he knew was the mortgage business and nothing else.

Albert couldn't comprehend that this could become a life-death problem. He might lose his law license. He would almost certainly lose his mortgage business. He might spend a little time in jail. If he ratted out what little he knew, they might break his legs. *So what?*

As his mind cleared, he began to develop the idea that they might be interested in Sam. The police were on TV looking for information. Albert could identify Sam and his partner. At least that was drug related. Apparently, the cops really wanted to ID Sam. That had to be worth something.

During the time Albert was in a drunken stupor, Boss received word from Victor that Albert had been arrested on a drug charge and released on a ten-thousand-dollar bond. The information he had received was that he had not done any talking so far. He was arrested with his girlfriend in a drug sting. The problem is that they don't know where he was getting his drugs. It could be from his girlfriend or some other source.

"Victor, did George read the riot act to Albert about his drug habit?"

"Yes, sir, Boss. George made it clear that he had to remain in control and we in fact limited his access. He was told not to buy drugs from any other source."

"Our problem, Victor, is that we have to notify Boston. I think we may need to handle this with outside help. Boston is getting nervous and we can only hope they don't get too uptight. From their point of view, things seem to be coming unglued. If things get too tight, Boston will simply move operations out of the area for the time being. You and I don't need that to happen."

Boston was discovering this very problem when they received the call from Boss. They all knew that Albert would eventually talk and this would lead the authorities to George, provide a tie-in with Reed and from there the situation would become very fluid. Number One informed Boss that the situation with Albert would be handled, hopefully before he could do any real damage.

Boss and Victor were not comforted. They both knew that their operations could be shifted elsewhere and they would be moved to another area or even out of the country until matters cooled down.

Unknown to Boss, Boston had already sent a text to Angel, who maintained his headquarters on a fifty-foot sailboat that he kept docked at various locations in the Yucatan. At the time of the message, Angel was docked at Isla Mujeres, off the coast of Cancun. Angel boarded a water taxi and within the hour of the text, he was purchasing his ticket to Atlanta, Georgia.

Angel arrived in Atlanta at two-thirty p.m. Eastern time. Boston had a private plane waiting for him and at three-forty five local time, he landed at the private airport in Crestview, Florida. At four p.m. Central time, Albert opened his front door to Angel, who, without preamble, shoved Albert back into the room, put his 9mm Glock against his head and said, "Have a seat in that big chair of yours, Mr. Albert. You and I have a little business to transact. We don't have a lot of time here, so why don't you tell me everything you told the police—and I do mean everything."

Albert stalled for time, but Angel would have none of it. He pulled a plastic bag from his pocket, walked over and put Albert in a headlock. When Albert was totally subdued, he slipped the bag over Albert's head. When

Albert was close to passing out, he was allowed to take a breath and then the bag was again used to cut off his oxygen.

Albert struggled, but it was useless. Angel was dressed in material that wouldn't shed and basically protected him from incidental injury. After a couple of rounds of this torture, Albert began to talk. Albert admitted that he had identified Tall Sam but no one else. He was holding out for a better deal before he identified Sam's friend. He had told them nothing about his business because they were only interested in the drugs. He didn't know much about Sam. He had made contact when he got his phone number and called it. He knew this was a number for a prepaid one-time phone. He gave this number to the police. He didn't know where these guys lived. If he wanted drugs, he would call that number and Tall Sam or his sidekick would show up.

Angel was confident he had extracted all the information he could from Albert. He allowed Albert to recover his wits about himself and then moved to a more friendly posture. "Albert, you've been helpful. If you hadn't been helpful, I'm sorry, but I would have had to hurt you a little bit. I'll tell the boys how helpful you've been. Maybe they'll take it easy on you. Here take this. I brought a little coke for you. I was told that if you were open and honest to give you some powder and then get my ass out of here."

"Thanks," said Albert. "To be honest, I thought you were going to kill me for awhile there. I really don't understand the big problem. I'm the one in trouble with the police, not you guys. What do I know? I know the mortgage business, but I don't know enough to get anybody in trouble. I know George and I knew Reed, but that's not enough for you guys to kill me. I'm not going to tell anybody about that mortgage business and get myself into even more trouble."

"That's good, Albert. My job is to make sure you understand that if you disclose anything about the mortgage business or even admit you know George or Reed, you're in some very deep shit. You understand?" asked Angel.

"Yes, sir, I surely do. You can tell them they have nothing to worry about. My lips are sealed."

Albert sniffed up the first bag of coke and then got into the Jack Daniels. Angel passed more coke to him and kept feeding him Jack Daniels. As Albert began to lose control, Angel started feeding him the potent stuff. It didn't take long until Albert went into shock. Angel laid him on the floor, pried open his mouth and dumped the contents of a bag of powerful coke into Albert's mouth. Angel slid a plastic bag over his head and death came quickly. Angel made sure Albert was dead, then he policed the area making sure he left no fingerprints or any other evidence he had been there except for the drugs.

It looked like Albert had overdosed on cocaine and bourbon. Either he choked to death on the cocaine or it put him into shock and killed him in overdose fashion. Angel had actually seen druggies OD in exactly this same way, except for the plastic bag. His personal choice would have been to shoot his guy and then burn the place down. The bosses wanted it to look like an overdose and it was their dime.

Angel got back into his car and drove to the private airstrip where the plane and pilot were waiting. Angel caught the eleven-fifteen flight out of Atlanta and was back on his boat in Isla Mujeres for breakfast the next morning. Albert was not discovered until one of the DEA men came to check on him two days after his death.

The officers checked the house and simply closed the case. It was obvious that Albert, distraught with guilt, simply took himself out in a blaze of glory. Hell, he couldn't stuff the cocaine in his mouth fast enough. They were impressed with the quality of the cocaine that killed him.

As the DEA team sat around headquarters that night, they were a pissed-off bunch. Albert had given them the name of the perp killed by Suzy and the phone number he had used. The phone number was no longer active and they virtually had nothing but the name of a dead perp. They found no record of this guy. They didn't know where he or his friend lived. They didn't know his friend's name. This turned out to be a dead end for the DEA team.

It took a couple of weeks for the news to make its way through to Heath and eventually to Chic. The information passed on to Chic was that some lawyer disclosed the name of the perp killed by Suzy. He turned out to be a petty crook known as Tall Sam. The name of his partner was unknown. They didn't know where Tall Sam lived. They had not found his fingerprints on record. They did believe, however, that since they had his name and a photograph of his tattoo, they would eventually get some useful information.

After trying to piece all the disparate facts together for a couple of days, Chic inquired about the name and location of the lawyer. It took another couple of days for the information to finally come back to him that the lawyer's name was Albert Barnes and that he was dead from a drug overdose.

His first impulse was to note how strange it was that people who had information he needed in the case tended to die before he could get to them. *What demon is following me around and protecting its children in this case?*

— 21 —

Chic realized that every complicated case eventually reaches a place where nothing seems to work. Every clue went down a dead-end path. Facts didn't fit together. Investigators became preoccupied with other cases. This case was particularly prone to hit dead spaces since he was the only guy actually looking for this phantom criminal conspiracy. He had plenty of murders and deaths that seemed unrelated to one another. Heath was helping him, but there was no unified team dedicated to solving the mystery and therefore, the chances of information getting lost in the system were higher. In fact, the only mystery was who killed these people. As to the existence of a syndicate that would tie all this together, the real mystery was why he thought there was such a syndicate. His patient load, time with Suzy and his concert schedule didn't leave him much time for this case during a two-month stretch.

Chic did, however, devote enough time to the case to know that Heath needed to search Albert Barnes' house, office, business checking accounts, as well as any safe he may have had in his house or office.

Chic dialed Heath on his cell phone. "Heath, this is Chic. How are you doing?"

"Doing great, Chic, but I don't really have any new information on the case," replied Heath.

"I've been thinking about that lawyer, Barnes. He's been dead about two weeks now, so I hope it's not too late to search his home and office. Do you think we can get a search warrant?" asked Chic.

"We don't really have anything on Barnes except that he was busted for drugs. We have the information that he bought his drugs from Tall Sam. The only information we have on Tall Sam is that he tried to kill Suzy and that he was a small-time drug dealer. We have no information that Tall Sam was involved in the murders of Gertrude and her friend. So what can we tell a judge that would allow us to search his home and office?"

Chic responded, "It's my opinion that Reed's death was related to information in his safe. The safe was stolen from Thomas Reed and then stolen from Gertrude, who was likely killed by Tall Sam. That means there's some correlation between Reed, the safe, the information in the safe, the death of Gertrude and the attempt on Suzy's life by Tall Sam. The attempt on Suzy was an effort to eliminate a possible witness. Barnes had a relationship with Tall Sam. While we can't prove that Albert Barnes' death was a murder, we do need to further investigate his death in order to eliminate that possibility. The only way to do that is to more carefully investigate the scene and to examine all the records we find to see if there's a stronger connection to Sam. In other words, we need to find out if Barnes had any connection with entities that were behind Tall Sam's possible activities as a hired killer.

"There's no doubt that Sam had help in Gertrude's murder. In fact, in my opinion, Sam was a hired gun. This entire episode bespeaks of a large organization—not just Sam and his partners in crime. We can explain to the judge that while we were able to trace some of Reed's business connections, the chief and DA are unwilling to devote many resources on this because they have an open and shut case against the ninja killers. We can tell the judge we believe the information we are seeking from Albert Barnes may dovetail with Reed's information and then lead us to the parties behind this spate of murders.

"And, let's face it; we'll have to find a judge with enough curiosity to want to at least eliminate Barnes as having information that might lead to the source of the murders. My sources tell me a lot of the local lawyers are curious about how he got rich in his little law practice in such a short time. If the lawyers are curious, I know the judges are equally curious."

"You're probably right about that," said Heath. "I know the lawyers in the area pretty well and I've heard a little undercurrent about Barnes getting wealthy overnight. It's my understanding that he hasn't inherited any money. He certainly isn't a trial lawyer, so he didn't get any large verdicts. He has very few clients. He operates without a full-time secretary. He does some loan closings, but the folks at the courthouse rarely see him.

"The strangest part is that he brags a lot. He claims he has some big out-of-town client who's making him a lot of money. He keeps hinting that he's come up with some new financial plan that this big client likes, but it was all a mystery that he couldn't reveal due to a non-disclosure agreement. I get the idea that the legal profession thinks he's just full of shit. They can't deny, however, that he recently came into some money from somewhere."

"Well, Heath," replied Chic, "I believe we can put together an affidavit that will get us the necessary search warrants. We have more than mere speculation about some wild conspiracy theory. You don't just gain the kind of money Barnes had out of thin air. There's something illegal going on here and we need to find out what."

Heath made contact with the local DA and he and Chic explained everything they had in the case along with Chic's view of the limited evidence they had collected.

Buster, the local DA, was not overly impressed with the relevancy of anything Albert Barnes did that was remotely related to Chic's criminal enterprise theory.

"Look," said Buster, "you really don't have much to go on here. The only reason I may go after the search warrant is that I became a little interested in Albert's activities myself. As a lawyer, he stunk. He didn't have many clients and I'd rarely see him in court. His recent rise in wealth raised a lot of eyebrows. We heard he was bad about being wasted on drugs, but we know he wasn't a dealer. The rumor was that he was involved in some big real estate venture. Nobody believes he was smart enough to make any money in real estate. Basically, the feeling around here was he was up to no good.

"You know the routine, Chic. Criminals will invariably get to a point where they have to brag about their exploits. This is especially true where some think they've outsmarted the system."

"I agree with that," said Chic. "Sooner or later, the urge becomes overpowering to let all those people who think you're stupid know just how smart you are. This desire overcomes the need to keep your mouth shut. Even in death, your life becomes an open book. Here we have a poor lawyer with no notable business that would support his new lifestyle. The money came too fast and the lifestyle changed so quickly that his peers noticed the difference. The other lawyers know from experience that this only happens when there's some illegal source of income."

Chic continued, "I have a strong opinion that the search warrants will reveal the nature of his illegal activity and that this information will lead to the sources of our local crime wave."

Buster looked at Chic with his silly half-grin and poked a little jab. "Now, Chic, you know that all these professional profilers don't believe in impulsive decisions in criminal matters. They say that impulse is unreliable and usually wrong."

"Actually, Buster, with most of them, I know I wouldn't rely on their impulses either. Most of them are tone deaf. No common sense. They don't have the touch. As far as I'm concerned, you have to use the facts along with your common sense. You have to be in touch with your inner voice, which speaks to you on a level we usually can't verbalize. We have to rely on our experience as human beings."

"Damn, Doc, you sound like some witch doctor," said Buster. "I bet your buddies give you hell about relying on some paranormal level of communication."

"Well, Buster, we do have some interesting conversations about the ability we possess to communicate on a nonverbal level and about where we believe impulses surrounding facts come from. If we get our minds out of the pigheaded belief that the human psyche can be analyzed on a purely scientific basis, then we can start to understand that human beings communicate on many different levels. We can begin to look at the power of faith and religious belief to affect the physical body.

"Buster, let me ask you a question about the power of suggestion and belief. I know you've had experience with voodoo and shamanism. I know we had that case a couple of years ago where the defendant was tried on three separate rape cases and each time he brought his shaman into the courtroom to somehow cast a spell on the jurors. Of course, it didn't work. And I know you had one case where the shaman put a curse on you. What did you learn from those experiences?"

"What I learned was that it would be very easy for certain people to actually believe in witchcraft," Buster said. "I've seen defendants who believe they were under a spell and no amount of persuasion would convince them otherwise. In fact, you may not know, but when that bunch put a curse on me, I had bad things happen at both hearings.

"The first hearing was on the day I found out my wife had cancer. On the day of the second hearing, a tornado blew down my house. That house was over one hundred years old and had never suffered any storm damage. At one point there, had I been so inclined, I could have easily believed that I was truly cursed. When we finished with the trial, I knew the judge had some grave dust given to him. We sprinkled a little around for good luck. We had a good laugh and I gained a wild tale to tell."

"I've seen enough," said Chic, "to convince me that voodoo is very real to some people. For example, how do we prove you were not cursed? If we look at this empirically, I doubt we could prove that psychiatry or psychology is any more effective than witchcraft at changing human behavior. To the believers in witchcraft, the shaman will have as much of a measurable outcome as a psychiatrist or psychologist with their believers. Mind over matter is a real thing. In the realm of the mind and human behavior, belief, faith and trust are the basic ingredients to a successful outcome."

"Chic," interjected Buster, "some people I know would accuse us of talking a lot of psychological bullshit, but whatever. I'm going along with the request for the search warrants. We would both be negligent in our duties if we didn't chase things to their logical conclusions. We'll prepare the affidavit and warrants by tomorrow. Check back with me around two p.m. and we'll go see the judge."

The judge signed the search warrants and authorized the subpoenas on Albert Barnes' house, office and safe, as well as to the bank where he kept his personal and firm accounts.

Albert had no close relatives in Florida. His girlfriend knew Albert had a cousin in Lincoln, Alabama, who would occasionally drop in on Albert. She contacted his cousin, Frank, who came down and got Albert buried. He was able to find Albert's will, locate the burial policy and accomplish some other basic business. Frank couldn't stay long, so he locked up the property and returned to work. He forwarded the will to an aunt in Atlanta, Georgia, named as Albert's executrix.

None of the relatives had bothered to come in and remove anything from the house and therefore everything was pretty much in place. The police had not disturbed anything much, seeing there really was no need. It was obviously an overdose case. The officers had searched for other drugs, but the place had not been trashed.

The trust account turned out to be the most interesting—and in fact, a mystery. There was one hundred ninety-two thousand dollars in the trust account, which looked like it was built up with many deposits under four thousand. The deposits were apparently cash. It had taken only a short three weeks to build up this amount. Going back some three years, there were consistent deposits amounting to over twenty-one million dollars. The records revealed that prior to three years ago there was very little activity in this account.

It took Chic several weeks to accumulate the records, which showed Barnes had made approximately three and a half million dollars in the last three years from this one activity. It was clear that this was some mortgage scheme, designed to wash money.

Chic was able to place the names with the mortgage payouts to the sellers. He checked the names and properties against the public records and found that none of the mortgages were recorded. It became obvious that the names were bogus, the mortgagors didn't own the property and the entire operation required a lot of cash money and a lot of organization. It also required a crooked lawyer.

This entire scheme shouted out "money laundering." This level of activity required a criminal enterprise with a lot of resources. The twenty-one million in cash put in an attorney's escrow account in amounts that didn't require reporting to the feds was a central part of the plan.

Chic was able to correlate a few names in Albert's office with names recovered in Reed's files. The names of a couple of loan companies appeared in both sets of records. Chic identified a couple of handwritten notes that referenced a guy named George. Beyond that, the trail of fraudulent names and addresses was impressive. Phone numbers were no help, as they were all bogus. Apparently, communication in this business was face to face.

Chic had seen enough to conclude that his hunches had been right. There was a conspiracy and he was getting a bad feeling about where this was leading. This was one he knew he would have to consider carefully and he would have to proceed with deliberate speed.

Chic was not his usual cheerful, lighthearted self that night. He was deep in thought. Suzy noticed his mood and with the skill of an accomplished vixen was able to move Chic to another state of mind. By the time Chic realized this transformation had occurred, he was already under the spell of this lively magician. Chic could only smile, as he was living proof of the power of the mind and the ability to cast a spell in the hands of the master craftswoman.

Further south in the inter-coastal waterway, Boss was cruising east in the direction of Panama City. He left his berth in Pensacola and picked up George and Victor along the way. Each had dropped anchor in Fort Walton, close to the city dock where it was convenient to board the yacht in the dark of night. Free from prying eyes and big ears, the group proceeded east to Choctawhatchee Bay where they decided to anchor out for the night. Boss loved to anchor out in Choctawhatchee Bay. It was big enough to offer privacy, but small enough for him to get to the entertainment in Destin. *Great food, great women, great beaches—what more could you ask for?*

Boss liked to anchor in the area near Crab Island where all the water activity took place. The best porn show Boss ever saw was right there near the bridge. Boss lay on top of his boat at dawn and looked over at the boat next to him and there sat a girl in the captain's chair, her lover standing in front, performing his manly duties. What a show! When they had spent themselves, Boss stood and gave vigorous applause. The two took a stately bow and disappeared below deck.

Tonight was not going to be that kind of experience for Boss. A dark moonless night for dark business. The men gathered around the table in the main salon, drinks in hand and dark expression on their faces.

Boss opened. "Men, here's where we are. Everyone is convinced that Albert overdosed on drugs. Tall Sam got himself killed when he underestimated Suzy. Chic and the police are searching Albert's records, which are going to expose us one way or another. They're going to be able to establish a connection between Sam, Albert and our small loan companies. This will get them to both of you. Then they might be able to tie us all together."

The band of happy warriors carefully analyzed the situation and concluded that what the police would find would be the legal side of their operations. All public records were associated only with the legal transactions. This was their carefully devised business model. Strong, legal business, financed via a daisy chain of corporations funded by drugs and other off-line sources. To crack the code, the police would have to negotiate the daisy chain of out-of-state and out-of-country private banks and nonprofit corporations. They were more vulnerable to discovery through the drug trafficking activity. This could be handled by letting the day-to-day operations be taken over by the Mexican cartel. As the fast and furious sting had proven, the federal government was inept at piercing the Mexican cartels.

Their response should therefore be in the nature of regular business guys being picked on by the authorities. After all, they couldn't be responsible for other people's illegal activities. Their loan business was valid, secured and recorded on the public record. They had nothing to hide. They felt confident that this would work for a while. They could see no way the police would ever prove they were involved with any murders.

Time came for the call to Boston. No doubt, Boston had a good grasp of exactly what was going on. The conference call was placed on the secure, encrypted line. They had enough relays in this process to defeat any prying ears. "Boss," announced Number One, "are George and Victor there?"

Victor and George both answered, "Present."

"Good. My associates, Two and Three, are here, so we're ready for your report."

Boss reviewed the entire situation, beginning with the death of Thomas Reed and coming up to the present time. Victor and George gave their view of the facts and then each gave their summary of their weaknesses. Boston gave their view of the matter, which basically agreed with Boss and Victor. The difference was that Boston was in charge of the game plan.

Number One cleared his voice and after a few words of praise for the group's discipline, he went into his summation and orders.

"Gentlemen, we have to conclude that the authorities will eventually determine that the local operations are at least in the money-laundering business. It will be difficult to tie us to the murders, but we must protect the core business. Essentially the local phase of our operation will have to be closed. We will have someone there shortly to collect all the cash and liquid assets you have in the safe. We'll leave two hundred fifty thousand cash, which should take care of immediate operating needs. Make sure all the assignments of mortgages are executed and all transfers of management agreements are signed. The only thing actually in house should be pending closings. These we'll fund through our legitimate working partners. When they check you out, Boss, we want this to look like a pure mortgage company on one side and a real estate management company on the other so you're not holding any assets unrelated to those businesses. Now you have mortgages on all your personal property and boats and so forth through our offshore company, so when we transfer funds, you draw on those loans as needed."

Boss listened carefully and confirmed that all matters were covered. Boston would leave George and Victor in place as bona fide small-loan companies. The large operation handled by Boss was intentionally designed to be a functioning mortgage company, which could be handled out of any of the regional centers. The management company would have to remain local but could easily be assigned to independent companies. At present, the assignment had been made, but Boss was to handle management in his office during the transitional period.

The plan in place, Boston ended the conference call.

Boss, Victor and George continued into the night like the well-oiled machine they were, in an attempt to polish off the sow's purse and transform it into the silk purse imagined. One thing all sociopaths understand better than normal humans is the nebulous nature of reality. People see what they want to see. They hear what they want to hear. With a little help, you can make the masses believe the mirage is reality.

Boss, Chic, George and Victor were all staring at the same harvest moon, which rose during the time of the meeting to deliver a beautiful night for them to behold. Each with his own thoughts revolving around the same series of events gazed at the same evocative sky. Only God in heaven could truly countenance the disparity of the views emanating from these four human minds on that night, which was truly a gift from God.

Chic, being the mystic he was, wondered if the other people involved with these events were all staring at this moon and contemplating their fates at this very moment. *Could he know this? Was he receiving some metaphysical message from these people who were totally unknown to him?* Chic had learned not to fight these thoughts when they entered his mind, as though he was nothing more than a conduit. There is that separate side of life that defies the technicality of the physical world, but that is as real as the physical side of life we see and feel. In the spiritual world, you have to exercise faith and at the same time apply a sober dose of logic. All humans essentially have this common experience afforded to them as living creatures in God's universe. Chic reminded himself that common experiences leads one to know the possible and the impossible, the likely and the unlikely. Chic accepted that some people are more gifted than others with sensitivity to the messages emanating from the mind and soul of other humans. There are times when you can sense this wave of energy and other times, only silence. Tonight the message board was flickering brightly in Chic's receptors. He could sense that the people involved were plotting their next move as surely as he was plotting his. What Chic felt was a moving target, which by fate continued to elude his grasp.

That night, Chic had that which every normal human experiences at some time: a message that no matter how hard you try, the golden ring is just a fraction too far to reach. It's the kind of dream that drives you to awaken— the kind where you are happy to wake up so that you can shake the frustration from the dark corners of your mind.

Boss, Victor, George and Chic, each in their private place with their private thoughts, looked at the harvest moon. From the depth of their souls, there arose a feeling of foreboding. The full moon, colored as blood, resonated somewhere in the lizard part of the brains of these men. They could sense the hot breath of the werewolf. Whose blood? Whose fate had been sealed in crimson this very night?

— 22 —

Heath received the call from the police chief that they might have a break in Tall Sam's case. Heath got Chic and drove over to Pensacola to the main police station.

"Good to see you, boys," said the chief. "We've made some progress in identifying Tall Sam. We got his name from Albert Barnes, who unfortunately died before we could pick his brain. Our contacts in the drug community told us he had a partner, a short guy named Fred Little. We couldn't find any criminal record for Sam, but his buddy Fred was a felon with a long record of theft, robbery and drug related charges.

"It's rumored in the community that these two were contract guys for some big banker in Pensacola. They tended to get drunk and run their mouths about being big-time assassins. Nothing specific, just general bragging about how important they are. You know the type.

"The DEA has run into Fred and knows him as a small-time dealer. They know where he was living six months ago, but they've lost track of him since."

"Chief," said Heath, "do we have any photographs of Fred that we can put out to the television channels with a 'wanted for questioning' message?"

"Yes, we can do that. I'll get that to the news media right now."

As soon as Heath and Chic left the chief's office, the chief contacted the news media, including all the television stations from Panama City to New Orleans and up to Dothan, Alabama. A lot of calls were coming in, but none that helped locate Fred. It was encouraging, however, that many of the callers recognized Fred although they had no idea where he lived. The positive news was that all the sightings were from Mobile to Panama City. The bad news was that no one had seen him in the last two weeks.

Heath and Chic both had run enough criminals to ground to know that most of them are creatures of habit. Like a bird, they will eventually come back to the nest. Fred's nest had to be in that area between Mobile and Panama City. Chic was confident that Fred would not stray far from home. Chic would wait. He needed Fred to get him off dead calm in this case, toward some meaningful resolution.

Fred was feeling the heat. Sam's death had rattled him and he had gone into hiding. He knew the cops were on his ass, but he really went off when he saw his picture on the television. If they wanted him for questioning, they must have some information about the killings. Like a cornered rat, Fred disappeared to his favorite hiding place.

He figured they'd never find him out there in the woods. There was no better place to get lost than up one of those creeks in his small fishing boat. There was plenty of food and water and that was all he needed. If he needed fuel, he could steal that from any number of boats in the area.

After several days of smoking pot, drinking moonshine, all mixed with a little meth, the demons within Fred took control. To say Fred became an animal was an insult to the animal kingdom. The meth reduced Fred to a demonic, beastly death machine.

Heath and Chic had accompanied the police to Fred's last known address. The place was deserted and had obviously been abandoned for several weeks. A search of the place was a waste of time, but as they were walking back to the car, Chic noticed a couple of 7mm casings in the yard. Probably not of any use, but Chic picked up the shells and put them in an evidence bag. Chic and Heath went back and searched the house and yard for other shell casings but didn't find any more.

The neighbors in the area confirmed that both Tall Sam and Fred had lived in that house for a couple of years. They stayed to themselves and didn't intermingle with the neighbors. The neighbors did report, however, that sometimes they'd go back into the woods and do some target shooting. They had never seen them shooting in the front yard. So how those shells got there was a mystery. Chic guessed that they cleaned up all their shell casings because he and Heath looked again and found no other shells or other evidence of target practice. The two casings they found must have dropped out of a sack or box in the process of moving.

Heath and Chic were headed back to Fort Walton on I-10 when the call came in over Heath's radio. Some crazy, wild man had just robbed a filling station on Highway 98 and was headed in the direction of I-10. The road the wild man was on intersected with I-10 about two miles east of Heath's present location. Heath and Chic were in perfect cut-off position and were the only cops within ten miles of the perp. Heath put on his blue lights, hit the siren and gunned the car toward the intersection.

Reports were still coming in. Apparently, this man charged into the service station wild-eyed, unshaven, ripped clothing and riot shotgun blasting. The store clerk was killed, along with two customers. The wild man grabbed the money from the cash register and robbed the dead bodies of their valuables. Bursting out the front door, he shot two people pulling up in a car for gas. A fifteen-year-old boy saw the whole thing. He escaped by jumping in a retainer pond before the guy could shoot him. The boy, however, got a few pellets in his back as he lay low under the water. The wild man jumped into his car and headed north with tires squealing. The young boy said it sounded "like a racing car gunning it down the raceway."

The dispatcher notified Heath that the suspect was probably Fred, the man they were looking for. Hearing this, Heath turned to Chic. "Chic, climb back to the backseat and get the assault rifle along with several clips of ammunition. You're riding shotgun. While you're back there, give me the Glock and hand me some extra clips. This is going to be a real ball buster! This guy Fred is from Dahlonega, Georgia and he knows something about driving cars. Those boys in the back hills of Georgia are trained from an early age how to drive a race car and how to avoid the police. They can build a race car from scratch, but can't read at the first-grade level. Get ready for a life-death fight. We're going to make sure it's him and not us."

"You got it," Chic said. "I'm ready. Let's go get this asshole."

"How about a little Beethoven on the radio to get us revved up?" asked Heath.

"Quit the funny stuff," said Chic. "Just get me to the party on time and we'll take care of this monster."

As Heath approached the intersection, the wild man was gunning it up the ramp in his souped-up black Ford Mustang. The man had to be doing one hundred miles an hour as he hit Interstate 10. Windows down, assault rifle raised, the crazed driver shot two drivers on I-10, immediately causing mass confusion. The first car he shot somersaulted down the road, running two or three other cars off the road. The second vehicle, a tractor-trailer, lost control, crossed the median and ran headlong into a SUV in the westbound lane. The tractor-trailer obliterated several cars, ending in a pile of broken machines, dead bodies and a massive fireball.

Heath had to leave the paved portion of the highway to get around the big pileup. He was able to maintain control, but by the time he got back to the paved portion of I-10, the Mustang was at least a half-mile away, probably hitting at least one hundred thirty miles an hour.

There wasn't time to do a lot of talking on the radio, but Chic gave their milepost and a report of the big pileup. That enormity of carnage would occupy the ambulances and police for hours. The next major intersection was in Crestview. Police from Crestview were on I-10 headed west. Hopefully Heath and the police could pin the Mustang in a vice.

Heath floored the accelerator but was making no headway on the Mustang. As they passed an intersection, the Mustang suddenly swerved left and managed to cross the median—quite a piece of driving. The driver moved out onto the westbound lane and promptly shot a couple of drivers, once again causing mortal hell to break loose. As traffic piled up, the Mustang was able to get to the exit west of the carnage.

Chic realized that the crazed maniac had managed to close the interstate to both east and west traffic, including blocking the officers headed in his direction from Crestview. Every ambulance and law enforcement officer in the general area would be totally consumed with the emergency for many hours. The Mustang was able to get off the interstate and head north to parts unknown. Chic and Heath were the only officers with a chance of finding and stopping this maniac.

Chic and Heath realized they were dealing with a maniac, out of his mind on drugs, who was smart, crafty and very fast on his reaction time. He was also a damn good shot and a superb driver. Somehow, Heath managed to avoid the carnage that was taking place on I-10 and could see the Mustang exit right on the Interstate. To this day, Heath cannot visualize how he managed to escape with his life in the midst of the mangled vehicles. Without a doubt, his training had delivered him on this occasion.

"Chic, keep that assault rifle ready. Flip it into automatic if you need to. Put that vest on. We've got a deadly situation here. No need to worry about being nice. Shoot to kill."

By the time they got on the two-lane road, the Mustang was almost out of sight. There were a few old dirt roads in this area, some leading up into Alabama and some off in the woods and into the bayou area. If they lost sight of the Mustang, they might never find him.

They wouldn't have the help of a helicopter and the likelihood of assistance was nil. This was going to be solo all the way.

"Heath, I think Fred doesn't want to lose us. I think he's going to try to lure us into some kind of ambush. He's crazy enough to try anything to get rid of his devils. At this moment, you and I are his devils."

"You might be right, Chic. He's staying just close enough to where we can still see him. He had a chance back there to totally lose us if he wanted to. He passed one car up there and didn't kill them. He knows where he's going and we don't. I think he'll turn off on one of these dirt roads and ambush us somewhere as we attempt to follow."

About five minutes later, Fred shot another driver as he passed him or her, which caused a spectacular crash. If the crazy man was trying to confuse them, he did a good job. They slowed to make sure that the driver looked dead so they could tell if there was any point in stopping to render aid. First priority was to stop the killing machine.

At this point, they had lost track of the Mustang. Heath was pushing the limits of safety on the narrow road and there was still no sign of the black Mustang. As they came over the crest of a hill, they noticed a little cloud of dust coming from a narrow dirt road leading off toward the west. They could see that a car had recently travelled that way at high speed. The skid marks indicated that he barely missed landing in the ditch.

"That has to be him," said Chic. "He shot that last guy to buy himself just enough time to set a trap. He's waiting on us somewhere." Chic consulted his GPS, which didn't show the dirt road, which was probably a good thing. At least they could assume that the road didn't circle back out somewhere.

"Slow up, Heath. To get out, he'll have to come back this way. Let's make sure we're ready for any ambush. He's crazy enough to just ram us head on."

Heath stopped and Chic got their head gear out of the trunk, checked their bulletproof vests, made sure they had their side arms ready along with their riot guns and assault rifles. The windows were down and their weapons could come into play quickly. Chic selected the .40 caliber pistol revolver and laid the riot shotgun with pistol grip next to him on the seat. Heath selected the thirteen-shot Glock with hollow-point bullets.

Chic, who was working with his new iPad, was able to confirm that the road they were on didn't circle back to the paved road. "Thank God for iPad and Google Earth," said Chic.

"Now you know I'm not big on the iPad, so show me what you're looking at," said Heath.

Chic showed Heath the surface map from Google Earth, which gave a clear image of the satellite view of the road and area where they were located. The maps and GPS agreed with the surface features. "Can't do much better than that," Heath said with a surprised look on his face. "I think I better add an iPad to my equipment." They confirmed that this road was not angling off in any direction that would take the Mustang back to the paved surface.

"Okay, Chic, speed is not our friend here. We have to go slow enough so we can react to any ambush. You get in the backseat so you can shoot out of either window."

The area was swampy and didn't afford many dry places for an ambush. The swampy ground also limited them to the surface of the road. They couldn't escape to the right or left without winding up in the swamp.

Heath and Chic agreed that the madman knew this area well. He was probably hanging out in his car alongside the creek. Heath's slow speed saved their lives. From the palmetto grove, Heath glimpsed the black flash headed directly at his door. He had only a couple of seconds to gun the car forward. The demon had calculated the impact at Heath's present speed, but Heath was able to jump the car forward so that the impact was in the trunk area. Chic jumped to the floorboard and was uninjured. Heath hit his head and was temporarily dazed. The Mustang had knocked Heath's car around in a circle, but Fred lost control and landed in the shallow swamp. Chic cleared out of the car with the riot gun ready. The madman was still in the Mustang but was not disabled.

As Chic was bringing his shotgun into position, the madman was trying to get his revolver into position to shoot Chic but was slowed down by the steering wheel. Chic fired before the madman could get his pistol in firing position. There wasn't much left of Fred's head. With the madman now relieved of his demons, Chic checked on Heath. Heath had a bruise on the side of his head, but otherwise was in good shape. The headgear had probably saved Heath from a serious head injury. Heath climbed out of the car, went over and surveyed the body of the mad dog. This would have to be a closed-casket funeral, for sure.

"Good shot," said Heath.

"Good driving," Chic said. "I think he figured he would hit right at your door, which would stop him from going into the swamp. He thought he would be on the road and we would be in the swamp. He was gambling he could then get out and finish us off before we could recover. Bad bet."

"Let's search the body and the car," said Heath.

"I'll check the car and body," Chic said. "Why don't you get on the radio and see what we can find out. We've got the tag number, so we ought to get a lead from that and at least confirm that this is Fred."

"Good idea, Chic. Frankly, I still feel a little weak. I probably need to sit here a little longer."

Chic waded out to the Mustang and began the search. To his surprise, the madman actually had his billfold in his pocket. Inside was a social security card in the name of Fred Little. They had hit pay dirt. On the other hand, Chic realized that once again, a key player was dead and with him, the information Chic needed to tie the murders to the money laundering to the individuals who were yet unknown. Chic thought of his dream—frustratingly close but no gold ring.

Chic and Heath were stuck there for several hours until a rescue team out of Pensacola was able to get down to them from Highway 90.

After the rescue vehicle arrived, Heath and Chic took the time to follow the trail to the bayou where they discovered the fishing boat where Fred had been hiding. The place was a total wreck with nothing of interest except the 7mm pistol. They suspected it was the one used in Gertrude's murder. This was later confirmed. The murderers who killed Gertrude and friend and who were after Suzy were dead. How many of the other homicides in the area were related to these two guys? They realized they'd probably never know.

On the positive side, Chic was impressed that the pressure put on by publishing Fred's picture on TV along with the death of his partner was enough to push this guy over the edge. The fact that Fred took a lot of innocent lives in his final fling with death, resulting in Chic killing him, had to be balanced against the deaths he would have caused had he lived.

How the pressure would affect the big boys in this operation was a matter yet to be seen. Chic began to develop a plan to apply pressure in the right place. So where was that pressure point?

The next day, Chic got permission to retain a title examiner to check all the public records, state and local, on all businesses whose name had been uncovered from the investigation of Thomas Reed, Gertrude Wade and Albert Barnes. Business licenses were to be checked along with the Internet. Chic believed this would at least lead him to businesses with common ties and names of individuals who would be subject to additional investigations.

It took about six weeks to get this information and a week or so of study for Chic to conclude where the pressure point was. At best, this was going to be risky. He might prove that various companies and individuals did business together, but so what? The public records did not prove or even lean toward illegal activity. Chic made his decision; he was going to apply the pressure and see what would happen.

It was the kind of decision that made Chic uneasy and made him question his judgment. Whether he was right or wrong, he was going to lose a friend. On the one hand, he would appear mean spirited and disrespectful. On the other hand, he was doing his job and protecting the health and safety of the public. In the end, Chic knew that he was going to follow duty first. He was compelled to do what he thought was right. *Is this the same kind of logic a hired assassin uses? Does the assassin just follow orders and do his job?* He wondered. *Well, the assassin may think, "I'm just doing the job I was paid to do. Knowing who the target is isn't my business and he probably deserves to die anyway."* Hopefully, Chic thought, what he was doing in the name of justice was acceptable in the eyes of God.

That night, Chic did his Bible study with Suzy and then took her to Pandora's for a good steak. Chic was moody and a little quiet. It was clear to Suzy that something was weighing on his mind. It took Suzy a little longer than usual to drag Chic from moody contemplation to his happy, lighthearted self. Chic accepted his decision and then let it go. It was time to forget his troubles and release himself to Suzy's tender care.

Suzy asked Chic how a drug-possessed person who was totally in a psychotic state of mind had enough sense to control a car and create a detailed plan of escape like the one this guy did. Chic finally worked up a smile and remembered an old joke about a smart maniac. Madman Fred had lent credibility to the old tale about a truck too tall to go under an overpass near the entrance to a mental institution. One of the mental patients was watching the driver who was too stupid to deal with the situation. The guy in the mental institution told the driver to let two inches of air out of each tire and then he could pass through. The driver looked at the person behind the fence and said, "That's pretty smart. What are you doing in the nut house?"

"I may be crazy," said the man, "but I'm not stupid."

As Chic lay in bed that night, the activities of the day began to focus his mind on all the innocent people who lost their lives at the hands of a maniac. *Life and death were difficult at best. Only in the arms of Christ, our creator, could there be peace.* Chic prayed for the souls of those who had died and for the families left with an incomprehensible void in their lives.

Had Chic known the details of Jack Beasley's story, the demons of the night would have been even more difficult to bear.

The trip from Atlanta had been wonderfully non-eventful. Jack Beasley got the family in his 2010 Ford Excursion at seven a.m. for the trip to Pensacola, Florida. The weather offered the kind of day you would order from Sears's catalog, if that were possible. The two kids, John, ten years old and Pete, twelve years old, were engrossed in their favorite cartoons. Thank god for DVD players in his Excursion. Between the movies and the games, travel with the kids was much less traumatic than it used to be. Every now and then, Beth would have to calm the kids down, but otherwise, life was truly worth living on this day.

Jack liked to drive. He could think better while driving than he could at the office. When Jack was sixteen, he worked at a grocery store where he spent his day checking out groceries. He found that repetitive tasks put him in the same kind of trance he was experiencing today. He could stay in that trance until somebody asked him a question about the change he had just given them. Driving had the same effect on Jack; he could fully function, but at the same time, drive for hours without any concept of time. He didn't consider it daydreaming because he knew he was fully alert as a driver, just as he knew he would make no mistake checking out groceries while in his dual state of consciousness.

Beth was asleep in the passenger seat and the traffic was flowing smoothly on I-10. Jack was still contemplating the fine meal they had at Hunt's in Dothan, Alabama. Best oysters he had ever had. He was really looking forward to all the great places to eat in and around Pensacola. When Jack was in the Air Force, he spent a lot of time at Hulbert Field near Pensacola. That area of Florida became his favorite place in the world.

As a thirty-nine-year-old guy, what more could he expect from life? He had a quality life as a navy pilot. He had seen the world. He loved his job with Delta. He had a beautiful wife who was smart, a great mother and not least, a really sexy gal.

His two boys were smart as hell. Both were better than average athletes. John was a rangy kid with exceptional hand-eye coordination. He was a natural at baseball and soccer. Pete took after Jack's father. Pete was built square with muscular legs, had great core body strength and was the kind of kid who commanded attention from other boys as a strong guy in both body and soul. He had the natural ability to end up a first-rate athlete at some college.

How lucky can a guy be? A man at peace with himself, his family, with the world and with God.

From the corner of his eye, Jack glimpsed what looked like two cars racing each other, headed in the eastbound lane of I-10. Jack's training immediately caused him to switch to combat mode. He quickly took in the westbound flow of traffic. He was boxed in with no place to go. He saw the exit about a half-mile west of his location.

As he looked for an emergency escape, in case he needed one, he saw the driver of the front car pull left as if he was coming across the median. At the same time, it looked like the driver fired shots at the vehicles to his right and to his front. All hell broke loose. Before Jack could process the utter mayhem that was unfolding, the last thing anyone in his SUV saw was the tractor-trailer coming directly at them across the median from the eastbound side of I-10. Mercifully, Jack's family was called to heaven quickly, without notice.

At the funeral, Jack's mother, Norma, could only ask how a loving God would allow something like this to happen. Her spirit morphed to that place where the only recourse is to frail away at the darkness. That place where anger sends the soul into the bottomless abyss.

Jack's father, Nathan, a man of faith, likewise had a sorrow that could not be expressed. The bottomless pit beckoned. Nathan was able to grasp that his son and family were in heaven. He found comfort in the arms of Christ, for he knew that Christ had removed the sting of death and gave victory over the grave. Death had taken their bodies, but their souls lived on. God's most precious and unique creation, the soul, could never be destroyed. As surely as the sun would rise the next day, he knew he would be united with Jack and his family in God's good time.

— 23 —

Another beautiful day and night in paradise, thought Boss. A couple of beauties had taken care of his physical needs and massaged his ego with big fat lies about how great he was. Boss would like to think he was great, but he knew it was the money and coke talking. For his part, he tried to remain under control and in charge.

While he liked to think he was in charge of his life, he knew better. He was a tool for the guys in Boston. He knew he was a prized employee. His knowledge of money laundering and creating a daisy chain was such that only the best investigator could penetrate the maze. The average peace officer stood no chance of penetrating his web of corporate entities, fictitious parties, charitable corporations and foreign banks. Boston liked his business plan.

In truth, he put the system into place, but Boston had other men who knew how to operate the system once it was set up. He probably had done too good of a job. He was no longer indispensable. He was fairly certain, however, that they needed him to manage the foreign banking operation located in Belize. He and Boston had developed two plans. One was an orderly transfer to Belize. He would simply board a plane to Belize and never return. This plan was scheduled to happen in two months, which was enough to look like a normal move, with an asset sale to a well-known real estate outfit. The transfers were already complete. The business actually operated as a skeleton at this time. If you got the company, it would be an empty bag—a sacrificial lamb, so to speak.

If threatened, he would exit by boat swapping over in international waters to a freighter and then he would eventually be dropped off in Belize. There would be no record of this transfer.

On the one hand, Boss was not happy, but on the other hand, he loved

Central America for its beauty and for the beautiful women. He was ready to take on the international banking operation. Everyone recognized he was the best-suited man for the job. He was truly satisfied, however, that he had helped create a nimble syndicate able to outmaneuver the police. When he got out of dodge, the police would be left with an empty bag and the syndicate would continue to operate as if nothing had happened.

The beautiful girls, the beautiful day, the good cigar and the unbelievable view from his patio couldn't totally assuage his concern that the vice was closing. Boston heard about the fiasco Fred caused just as soon as he had. Hell, this made national news. Everybody in the world knew what Fred had done. The only good thing about it is that Fred is dead and can't talk.

When Ken talked to Boston, they were not pleased. He didn't sense any change in their attitude toward him, but he was keenly aware of their rules against notoriety which emanated from the criminal side of the operation. Even though there was no way to connect Fred to him, Boston would at least consider laying this world renowned mass killing at his feet. Ken couldn't control those events, but he still had faith that his value to the company was enough to keep him alive.

Number one concluded the conversation with Boss, then turned his attention to Number Two and Three as they weighed the impact of Fred's killing spree on Ken's future with the organization.

"Gentlemen," said Number One, "we all agree that Ken is one of our brightest stars. We really don't need to lose him. He also is the primary weak link as the only remaining person who could connect us with the events in Florida. The question is whether or not this Chic guy can locate Ken and then somehow turn him against us."

Number Two, after a pregnant pause, spoke. "As you men know, I'm in charge of security, so it will probably come down to me to make that decision."

"You are right," said Number One. "We are going to discuss it for a while, but in the end it is your decision. We will stand behind whatever you decide on this."

"Well, I have to admit that we need to take Chic seriously," replied Number Two. "He's one man, but a dangerous man. In fact, in my case it has gotten personal. As you know, my wife graduated from Florida State. She was a beauty queen there. You know we met while on vacation with our families at the Breakers in Palm Beach, Florida. As soon as Chic made the world news as Fred's killer, she recognized Chic as the guy who has been the featured singer at an event put on by the Boston Symphony. She's heard him sing and is quite fascinated with him. Chic is also a graduate of Florida State. So, now I have to hear how great he is from my wife! If anyone can find Ken and have a chance of turning him, it's Chic."

"We are lucky we only have to worry about one part time investigator instead of the whole federal government. You know our friends from England just got hit with a two billion dollar fine for laundering money. We are not as big as they are, but we are big enough to attract interest if Chic uncovers enough of our operation," said Number Three.

"You're right Number Three, but you should also know that the feds didn't close down the English holding company. The government knows that the off line economy is so large that they can't afford to actually shut down the money laundering business," said Number One. "The very size of our business is, in fact, a form of fire wall. Number Two, this is your decision, so make it."

The meeting completed. The men were served their usual steaks with all the trimmings.

Sunday night, it was time for Chic to get ready to meet up with the Fish House Gang again. This was supposed to be the last time at Ken's house for a while. The group was going back to Harbor Docks for a season. This would take a little pressure off Ken.

"Chic, what do you rusty, old men do over there at Ken's, other than play cards?" inquired Suzy. "I hear tell there are women over there just to tempt you guys. Is that so?" Suzy locked onto Chic's eyes and said, "Now, Chic, you know I can read your mind, so don't lie to me."

"Ken does have a couple of girls serving the food. They do dress a little skimpy and they do a good job of teasing the guys, but that's it. We don't have any strip shows and we don't have any guys running off to the back room with the girls. This bunch of men would not allow that to happen."

"Go have a good time," Suzy said. "You need to lighten your mind of the burden of killing that guy. Have you ever had to kill a person before?"

"This was my first. I've had to subdue several men with physical force. I've had to hurt a few guys in the process. I've had to shoot a couple of guys, but I was able to simply wound them. There was no choice with this guy. He had already shot about ten people and several others died in car wrecks. If I had been a second or two slower, my head instead of his would have been blown off."

"So, here we are. This case has put the two of us in the position to have had to kill somebody within the last few weeks. How weird is that?"

"Weird," said Suzy. "Two killers sitting here smiling at each other like two teenagers. Are we normal?"

"I can't speak for myself as being abnormal, but I can assure you that *you* are absolutely abnormal. In a good way, I should add. The way you've been able to handle the entire ordeal has been an inspiration to me. You've taught this teacher a lot more about life than I've taught you. Thank you."

"Ah, quit it, Chic. You're just playing with me now."

"No, I'm dead serious. You've taught me a lesson and I appreciate it." Chic kissed Suzy and forced himself out of the house to go play cards with a bunch of old men.

The group was already eating by the time Chic got there.

Bob started the festivities. "See what happens, guys, when some pretty little redheaded gal gets in your breeches? You can't quit screwing long enough to come play cards with your friends."

"No, no," said the Judge. "Chic's been too busy bragging about blowing that madman's head off the other day to worry about Suzy."

"From what I hear," said Ralph, "we need to pat him on the ass for that one."

"Here, here." said Percy. "That was some bad ass. Wasn't he the one that killed Gertrude and it was his partner that tried to kill Suzy?"

"You bet," said Chic. "This guy was a true bad ass. We saw him shoot and kill about six people. I mean he shot them like dogs. If I had been a second slower, I would be dead. Heath and I are lucky to be here."

"This is one hell of an interesting situation," said the Judge. "Boyfriend, girlfriend, both kill a killer within a few weeks of each other. Now, that's a hell of a thing to have in common. How is Suzy dealing with having killed a man?"

"Better than I am," Chic said. "I told her tonight that she was an inspiration to me. She's handled the whole situation with stability and a calmness greater than I can muster. Now, this is a strange way of putting it, but if I'm in a fox hole surrounded by the enemy, she's the person I want in there with me covering my back."

"I'm with you, Chic," said Ken. "May as well die happy, rubbing asses with your partner in the fox hole."

All the guys agreed on that. Percy turned serious and said, "Look, Chic, you being a psychologist, a criminologist and a 'songologist,' what the hell gets in a man's mind that allows him to ride down the road killing people along the way? What in the devil is their motive? How do you get that desperate?"

"There's not a real answer to that question," said Chic. "Who really knows the mind of man? We can analyze statistics and arrive at patterns of behavior. We can do a lot of things, but trying to predict the actions of a single individual is still in the realm of the great unknown. I'll tell you this much, if you can imagine something in your mind that a human being can do to another, no matter how terrible, someone has already done it and someone else at that very moment is working on a better way to do it. What is it in the human condition that can explain how that's possible or explain what course of action can be taken that would stop that kind of behavior?"

"Well," said Percy, "I was hoping you had some good answer, but I can see there isn't an easy answer. To get an answer, you'd have to turn to the Bible and I know you so-called scientists don't like to do that."

"Percy," replied Chic, "I have to disagree with you on one point. I don't call what I do a science. The term 'social science' is, in my book, an oxymoron. We can study the physiology of the brain, the electrical patterns of the brain and the areas of the brain where certain functions take place and we can study the effect of drugs on all these physical and otherwise electrical elements of the brain. The behavior of individuals is quite another matter. But you're right; it's not accepted to quote the Bible as a source of authority in the field of psychology. I actually do look at the Bible as an authority in this area. In my view, many of the teachings of Christ are based on sound principles of human psychology and behavior. All of the parables used by Christ have meaning and application on several levels. They're practical lessons on how to live and they also convey a spiritual message about our relationship with God.

"You could easily believe that humans can be possessed by what can only be described as demons. You can certainly conclude that the wage of sin is death. The power of faith can't be underestimated. The concept of keeping your eye on the goal is as sound in sports as it is in religion. Man is capable of essentially returning to his animal roots and can act like a savage, wild beast.

"You can also look at the effect of money and wealth on the human psyche. Man will clearly sell his soul for what he thinks is financial security. I might add that it's the fate of many people to sell their souls very cheaply for the mere vision of wealth. Desire for wealth, security, power and excitement combined with drugs is the mother of much crime.

"Percy, I hope you know more about the subject than before you asked me the question. If not, you can share in my confusion."

Ken took over Bob's usual role of being the smart ass and chimed in with, "Hell, the devils make us do these things, so we can all remain in communal ignorance on the subject. Now deal the cards. I'm ready to take some money off you suckers."

As the cards were being dealt, the Judge had to add his two cents on the subject. "Now, you boys are missing the most important motivation in life. You know what I mean. It's pussy. There's never been a man that couldn't be lead astray by a woman willing to use her talent. Then they outlive us and end up with all the money."

— 24 —

Chic, Heath and the police chief met at their favorite Waffle House for a high-level meeting on their progress with the various businesses related to Reed. Chic had come to several conclusions after reviewing all the known facts.

"Man, I hope nobody minds meeting here at the Waffle House to discuss business," said Chic.

"The bums here this time of the morning are still hung over from last night," replied the chief. "I'm in street clothes, haven't shaved and we all pretty much fit in with the rest of these derelicts! We're safe as long as we follow the Waffle House rules. You two guys pass the test. Just keep your voice down."

After placing their orders, Chic began, "The only thing I've found that you may not know is what we've been able to determine from the public records and from Tall Sam, Fred Little and Albert Barnes' checking account and financial records. Barnes was acting as the attorney for a fraudulent mortgage scheme. Money was deposited in Barnes' trust account in lots of three to four thousand dollars so it didn't have to be reported. When the amount built up, they would have a bogus loan closing.

"Albert Barnes' records didn't reveal the true names of who was giving him the money. I could correlate the receipts to the names of the buyers, but those were all bogus names. He did keep some handwritten notes, which we found, that seem to correspond with deposits being made. We found a couple of references to Thomas Reed, one or two to George Currier and a few that mentioned Victor. Phone records show he called a loan company run by a 'George' and one by a man named 'Victor.' We can also correlate phone calls made to Tall Sam's number. We can tie some of these contacts to the dates of deposits and some to the dates of bogus loan closings.

"Of the entire bunch, it seems that only George and Victor are still alive. The first problem is we have no information that ties George and Victor to any of the killings. At this point, it appears all the killers are dead, so we stand little chance of tying the murders to the money-laundering business.

"As to the money-laundering business, we can show that Albert, if he were alive, would have eventually been in trouble with the IRS. We have enough information to warrant a close surveillance of the loan companies run by George and Victor. These two loan companies are tied to the mortgage company run by Ken Renfro, who's a friend of mine.

"Here, we have to be honest. All the business relationships between Ken's companies and the loan companies run by Victor and George are purely legal as far as what we see. We only have a suspicion that the two loan companies may have some off-line business connection with the bogus mortgage business. Ken may be totally innocent, but I have to admit that he meets the profile. He certainly has the necessary assets to run this kind of large money-laundering operation. I can't think of a local business that would fit the bill better than Ken's."

"Chic, do you think you can actually conduct an investigation of your friend and not get personally influenced one way or the other?" asked Heath.

"If I think it's clouding my judgment, I will certainly hand the investigation off to someone else. But I do know that in order to pull off the capers we've seen, it would require someone like Ken who has access to a lot of money. He has the gravitas to handle this kind of enterprise. If it isn't him, it would have to be his double. I'm going with my gut reaction, which is that Ken is the top dog here. The question is how do we smoke him out?"

The men kicked this around for quite a while before they settled on a course of action. The chief was going to call a friend at the IRS. There was enough there for the IRS to do an audit on the two loan companies.

The next leg was for the chief to commit to having three officers conduct surveillance on Ken, Victor and George. Chic would give the start time since the chief could only commit a total of nine days to this surveillance. The final piece was close communication between the three watchdogs and long-range surveillance equipment. They couldn't get a tap order, but other than that, they could use all their modern surveillance toys. Heath was in charge of the equipment and the electronic surveillance.

Plan in place, the men departed in high spirits. The hunt was on and the blood sport had begun.

As Chic departed the Waffle House, he thought of the many conversations he had with lawyers who reminded him that you should never be close friends with police officers. It was their position that if the lawmen ran out of something to do or out of leads in a case, they were likely to look at their friends with a gaunt eye. From this aspect, it was dangerous to be friends with a cop. Chic wondered if he was guilty of this façade as he turned his spotlight on a friend.

The following Tuesday, Chic made a surprise call on Ken at his office in Pensacola. He took the chance Ken was there and that he would take the time to talk to him. Chic came in the first-floor area where the staff worked and noticed they seemed more busy than usual. Chic asked the receptionist if Ken was in and she pointed Chic to the yacht.

Chic walked out the door to the motor yacht and observed Ken busily fidgeting around the boat. There was nothing like a boat to occupy a man's attention. It was the worst lover of all—demanding full attention, bottomless access to money and in return providing questionable pleasure.

Chic walked out to the yacht and hailed Ken. "Captain, can I come aboard?"

"Sure, Chic, come on aboard. Thinking about taking a little trip. Want to come along?"

"Wish I could, Ken, but not this time. I need to talk to you about a serious problem, if you have the time."

"Chic, if it's serious, I guess I better take a little time. What suit are you wearing today—doctor or detective?"

"I'm afraid it's detective. Not my favorite suit when I'm talking to a friend. I hope you understand that what I've got to say to you is in the spirit of concern and frankly has to be solely between the two of us. If some people I know hear about this, I'll be in a little trouble."

"Chic, I'm sure that nothing I've done will jeopardize you in any way. Don't beat around the bush. Give it to me straight. I hope some girl hasn't turned up pregnant."

"I wish that was it, but it's not. In fact, I don't know a good way to get into the subject, so I'm going to take your advice and just throw it out there.

"What's happening is that the FBI has developed an interest in the many murders that have been going on in the last several months. They feel like there's some RICO activity going on—you know, drugs, murder and money laundering, all tied to a national syndicate. I don't know if there's Mafia activity or not, but the problem is that they've identified your company as being tied to certain loan companies that may be tied to the lawyer Albert Barnes' death and to his bogus loan business."

"Hold it there, Chic. Are you telling me the FBI is on my tail and that I'm somehow connected to murders and RICO activity? I'm in the mortgage and real estate business and everything I do is a matter of public record."

"Ken, I don't have to tell you that once the FBI gets a sniff of a syndicate or mafia operation, it doesn't matter if you're guilty or not. In RICO cases, the net is wide and can ensnare a lot of innocent people. The FBI can and will break you one way or the other if they smell something fishy. They can isolate you from your friends. I don't know what they have on you, maybe nothing. What I do know is that you're a party of interest to them. They can put the IRS on your companies and generally make your life miserable. If they think you're part of a RICO enterprise, everybody you touch will come under suspicion. I hate to tell you this, but if you value your friends, including the Fish House Gang, you need to stay clear for a while."

"Why in the hell are you telling me this, Chic? Do you think I'm some kind of a Mafioso crook? What have I ever done to give you the idea that I'm a low-life like that? I guess if I'm that damn dangerous, you had better get out of here while you can. Before you know it, they'll have you before some board for helping a potential or suspected crook."

"In fact, Ken, you're right and this will be our last meeting until you're cleared. I'm here because you're my friend and I think I at least owe you a warning. I'm also here to tell you that if you have anything to hide, then now is the time to come clean before it's too late. I don't want to hear it, so if you decide you have information to disclose, you need to call Heath.

"Ken I know this doesn't sound very friendly to have a friend come suggest that the authorities think you're involved in some pretty hideous crimes, but I would hope that if the shoe were on the other foot, you would warn me."

"I do appreciate the warning," Ken said. "But I don't have the foggiest idea what I can do about it. I'm just a guy who's worked hard all his life to build his business and I've been very fortunate. My books are open and will withstand an IRS audit. I can't imagine why the feds think I'm involved in any illegal activity."

"I didn't come to accuse you," Chic said. "I only came to give you a heads up. That's as close as I can come to helping you without getting in deep trouble myself. Even if you're as clean as an angel's butt, they would find me guilty of interfering with an ongoing investigation and I would become as suspect as you would in any RICO conspiracy. I'm not here to get any confessions or get any more involved than I already am. I'm leaving the ball in your court when I walk off this boat. Take care."

Chic left Ken seated behind the helm. Chic could detect no real emotion from Ken. He sensed deep contemplation, but it was evident that the gears were turning at a very controlled speed. Practice is what Chic sensed. Chic knew that Ken was no stranger to stress. Chic had studied Ken's eyes and by the time he left, he was convinced that Ken was the guy in charge. Here was a man who could order his best friend killed and have absolutely no second thoughts. In fact, Chic was convinced that Ken could issue an order to kill, sit down at a lie detector and deny it and pass. There was coldness about Ken that Chic had not previously recognized.

Chic knew Heath had him under surveillance with his long-range directional mic, so he spoke under his breath as he walked away from the yacht basin, "Heath, if my instincts were admissible in court, we could convict Ken right now for murder, distribution of drugs and laundering money. Make sure everybody is in place."

Two blocks away, Chic met Heath at one of the downtown clubs where they could keep an eye on the yacht. Heath had a unit managing the communication van while he and Chic did the visual. "Didn't take long," said Heath. "Ken's on his cell phone making a coded call. The long-range hearing devices didn't pick up anything, so he made the call from a safe room on the yacht. The call only lasted ten seconds, so it had to be some kind of prearranged signal."

Chic got up to get a better view and when he did, he saw Ken untying the dock lines. "Heath, let's get ready to move. Ken is leaving in his yacht." Ken was already leaving out through the sea wall as they exited the café.

"Chic, we weren't planning on him leaving on his boat this soon. I guess we should have figured he used the yacht as a meeting place. If we followed him on the water, it would be way too obvious. Our listening devices can't really follow him, so we're generally deaf to his communications."

Ken was disappearing in the direction of the Gulf of Mexico when they received word from the two watchers that George and Victor had gone to their respective marinas and were now in their boats headed in the direction of the pass to the gulf. At this point, all three were out of Heath's range. All they could do at this point was wait and record their return time.

While they couldn't prove it, Heath and Chic knew they were meeting somewhere on Ken's boat plotting their next move. They could only hope that Ken and his associates reacted in a way that would disclose a weakness the police could exploit. An audit by the IRS would not take place for several months. They could probably get a search warrant for the two loan companies, but Ken was still not legally implicated.

Heath contacted the police chief, who was asked to contact the coast guard to pull a full search on Ken's yacht as he returned to the yacht basin. They were certain he was coming back, so it would be easy enough for the coast guard to stop Ken and do a full search of the yacht. The coast guard didn't need a search warrant, as Ken found out about eleven that night when he was within a mile of his office.

The coast guard tender came with lights flashing and megaphone operating. "This is the US Coast Guard. Heave to."

As they came alongside, the voice on the megaphone asked, "Captain, do you have any weapons aboard?"

"No, sir," replied Ken.

Three black clad men with automatic weapons in hand boarded the yacht. One placed Ken in a convenient position and commenced the interrogation. The search lasted over an hour. Every crevice and compartment was examined. Eventually, Ken was given a ticket for not having the correct signage in the head and in the motor compartment.

The officer in charge pulled Ken aside before they left and explained how he should personally call him if he saw any drug activity at the yacht basin.

"It's every boater's duty to turn in any person they see involved in drug activity. By the way, I didn't give you a ticket on this, but you need to clean up your engine room. It also looks like your radio license is not up to date. You got a yacht like this, you need to keep it ship shape."

"Yes, sir," said Ken. "We'll keep our eyes open. If I see any drug activity, I'll call you immediately. I hate druggies myself."

Ken was tired, so he took the boat to a safe anchorage and spent the night on the hook. Ken was pissed at Chic, but he did admire his style. The two of them would have made good partners in crime. He realized that he and Chic could look each other in the eye and lie with great ease. Ken knew without a doubt that this visit from the coast guard was not on impulse; they were there at Chic's request.

The time to depart was at hand. He took out his world phone and left a short encrypted code at a drop number. This drop-box phone answering machine was checked on a regular basis by Boston, who would get the message and activate the prearranged plan for communication.

Victor and George arrived back at their marina and their time was recorded.

On the third day of surveillance, Victor was seen in the company of a known drug dealer. The two met at a rest center on I-10 and the surveillance officer was able to get a good photograph of Victor and the druggie, as well as the tag numbers of their vehicles.

Victor exited his car with a box of Kentucky Fried Chicken and a drink. The druggie approached Victor at the table where he was eating and spread out his own Kentucky Fried Chicken and drink. The druggie was also carrying what looked like an old department store bag, which he slid under the table. The druggie left first, leaving the bag under the table. Victor left with the bag.

Heath was able to obtain the history of the known drug dealer. At this point, they had enough information for a search warrant of the dealer and Victor.

Heath and Chic met the chief at his office early the next morning.

The chief leaned back in his big chair and propped his feet up on his desk. "Boys, looks like we hit pay dirt here. We know now that Victor's in the drug business. The dealer has a long record and we can threaten him with life if we catch him with drugs. I say we arrest the asshole and threaten him with life unless he cooperates. This guy is a talker, so I bet he'll spill the beans. Once we arrest Victor, the cards will begin to fall."

Chic asked, "How soon can we get an arrest warrant for the dealer?"

"Actually," said the chief, "we have an alias writ on him from Alabama, so we can arrest him now, but I also want a warrant from Florida. It will help us hold him without bond. Come tomorrow night, this guy will be in jail. After a couple of days, he'll see the need to talk."

They agreed to focus the surveillance on Ken, since they didn't have the funds to extend time on Victor and George. They believed the arrest of Victor was close at hand and that he wasn't going anywhere.

The next day, the chief was good to his word. The drug dealer, whose name was Duffy Chappell, was arrested. Duffy was found to be in possession of over a pound of cocaine, a stock of meth, ten pounds of hash and several weapons. With his record, he was clearly looking at life. Duffy was a professional criminal and therefore understood that helping the cops violated the code of the professional criminals. His life would be hell in prison if he cooperated with the cops. He was certain that Victor's people would kill him if he got out of jail anytime soon.

It took a promise of witness protection and a lot of hard bargaining to bring Duffy around. Duffy clearly understood the value of the information he possessed. It took two weeks to reach an agreement with Duffy. He insisted on isolation from the general prison population. He had no doubt his life was in jeopardy. His limitation was that his information was confined to his dealings with Victor. He had no knowledge of Victor's connection with a syndicate.

— 25 —

Ken knew he was under surveillance. This made his communication with Boston a little more difficult. He needed to get to a location where Chic couldn't use all of his electronic devices to listen in on his conversations. Ken had received word that Duffy was arrested, but word from the jail was he had not opened up yet. Ken knew it was just a matter of time.

The weather was overcast and the night was pitch-black. Ken lowered the Donzi into the water from his home in Destin and blasted off into the Choctawhatchee Bay at high speed. There was no way they could follow him in that boat. He didn't turn on his radio or any other electronic devices other than the depth finder. With the depth finder and compass and a powerful spotlight, Ken could find his way to their safe house at Black Creek in Freeport.

Ken's concern was the coast guard. He knew they rarely operated late at night in this area. But if the coast guard knew what boat he was using, they could possibly spoil his escape plans. If he left from Destin in one of his boats, he would have to go past the coast guard station to get to the Gulf of Mexico. Ken knew he would have to revisit his escape plan.

Ken had sent a text message with a two-word code to Victor. Victor would be in his own boat waiting for him in Black Creek, in Freeport, Florida. Ken passed under the Highway 331 bridge and changed bearings to east-northeast toward the mouth of Black Creek. He passed over the shoal line and slowly motored a couple of miles to a very isolated cabin. There was no electricity in the cabin to contend with and it was only accessible by boat.

Victor was sitting on the screened front porch of the fishing cabin with Coleman lanterns providing the only light except for the occasional red glow of Victor's cigar. Ken tied off his boat and climbed up to the porch.

"Have any problem, Victor?"

"Nope. Everything went okay. I didn't see my tail anywhere. How about you, Boss?"

"They had me staked out, but they don't have a boat and even if they did, they couldn't have followed me."

"I don't know about that, Boss. That Chic is pretty handy with a boat, so I've heard, but even he couldn't sneak up on you at night out in Choctawhatchee Bay."

"Our problem, Victor, is how we get out of here without encountering the coast guard. If they know what boat we're in, we'll be an easy mark. I know they have me under surveillance, so all they have to do is follow me to the marina. We still have to come through the pass, so we would become sitting ducks."

"You know, Boss, this damn cabin is so isolated we could get lost right here on Black Creek."

"Not a bad idea," Ken said. "We could do exactly what we did tonight. Wait until daylight and have a helicopter fitted to land on water pick us up and drop us off on the freighter, which is going to be waiting on us some sixty miles out. We'll leave after twenty-four hours in our sea-going cigar boat and hightail it to Cancun. We can refuel and shoot on down to Belize. So far as I can see, we're ready to leave as soon as we can set this up—maybe two days at the most."

Ken knew he had planned well. He had a yacht stationed in Belize that was registered in Panama and that could be quickly sold for a couple million dollars. This was a common way to hide assets from the federal government. There was no way for the government to trace the title to him. The money from the sale would never reach the United States. This, along with the mortgage money on his property, would give him all the cash he needed until he got fully operational in Belize. Having Victor along would certainly make his life easier.

"Victor, plug your head jacks into this divider here so we don't have to put the phone on speaker."

Victor obliged and Ken placed the call to Boston on the encrypted world phone. Connection established, Ken announced that he and Victor were at "location zero." The triad was all there and Number One took the floor.

"Gentlemen, first let me acknowledge that our friends in the Sinaloa cartel have reviewed our situation and they're ready on their part and have approved our transfer. We understand that Duffy Chappell has been arrested but has not talked at this point. Basically, we need to act immediately. Is everything ready?"

"Yes, sir," answered Ken. "We have cleared out my safe and all transfers are completed. My office will simply cease to function. The records there are in order and support our position as a legal and legitimate business. All the documents and computers will lead only to legitimate operations. There will be just enough money in the bank to support current operations. The ladies in the office are only aware of the legitimate operations. Granted, my disappearance will look fishy, but people disappear all the time. What the authorities will get is an empty bag. Victor may end up with an arrest warrant on him, but nothing that will interfere with our international operation. He'll have a new identity in Belize."

"Very good, Boss." said Number One. "We have decided that there is no time like the present. We can activate the plan in the morning. The helicopter will be at your cabin at seven a.m. You will immediately be airlifted to a freighter approximately sixty miles out in the gulf. You know the plan from there. Is there any reason why you can't remain at the cabin until the helicopter arrives?"

Ken answered, "I'm ready. I kept my passport and a small bag of things I need on me for the last week so I could leave immediately. I'm ready to disappear. Do you have the new identification ready for us on the freighter?"

"Yes," said Number One. "Everything is in order."

"Victor, are you in position to leave or do you need to return home first?"

"Number One, I need to do a few things, but I'll be back and ready to go within six hours. I haven't been under surveillance for the last two days, so I shouldn't have a problem."

"Victor, the pilot has strict orders to leave no later than seven-fifteen a.m. If you're not there, you'll be totally on your own. I advise you not to get caught. You understand what I'm saying."

"I understand clearly, Number One. I will not be caught." Victor had no illusion about his choices.

The conference completed, Ken disconnected. "Victor," said Ken, "why do you need to go back home? If I were you, I'd stay right here. Why take a chance?"

"Boss, I still want my passport and I just need to get a few things. I don't want to leave a couple of my guns there either. They can't trace them to any murders, but I just don't want them left here."

"You're a big boy, Victor, so you know the risk you're taking. If you're not here, you'll be left. You've got plenty of time, so if you're going, get out of here now. What kind of GPS do you have?"

"I only have the portable one on the dash."

"Don't turn on your electronics, including your cell phone. Go get your GPS and the cell phone and I'll keep them here. If you're caught, I don't want anybody tracing you back here. Do you have any charts or other material referencing the location of this cabin?"

"No, sir," said Victor.

Ken decided that the safe thing to do was to go with Victor and check out his boat. Victor disconnected the radio, took the GPS and the cell phone and handed them over to Ken. He was cleared to leave.

The Boston triad continued their discussion of the situation in the Panhandle of Florida. The business operations in the region were transferred to Atlanta. There was no change in the drug operation. George had not been there long enough for the cops to really have anything on him. He should be able to direct the drug operation, especially with the active help of the Sinaloa cartel. The changes they had to make in Fort Walton were about like a mosquito biting an elephant's ass as far as this operation was concerned.

Number One spoke, "Gentlemen, we have concluded that the feds aren't actually interested in any detailed investigation. They don't see any grand scheme here. It's my view that the FBI doesn't have the kind of agents that are able to fathom the depth and breadth of our operation. We don't follow the pattern of the mafia. We're basic businessmen. We're in this for the money. We also know from experience that the feds haven't been able to crack our partners, the Sinaloa cartel. The Fast and Furious operation has proven this."

"Hear, hear," chimed in Numbers Two and Three.

"Now, I realize that we had originally planned on taking Ken out, but after careful thought, he's worth enough to us in our international monetary operations to save him. We will give him a new identity and put him to work in Belize. Fact is, we don't have another man as qualified as he is to handle that business. Do we all agree?" Numbers Two and Three agreed.

"Gentlemen, time to join our wives downstairs for cocktails and steaks and receive the adoration of our subjects. Are we ready to enter the world of black-suited shitheads?"

"You got it, Number One," the boys said in unison and away they pranced to the world of the common person.

In their own minds, they were gods of this world. They understood their position clearly. Most of the world considered successful men as somehow crooked. This triad knew that most businessmen were honest, hardworking, God-fearing, red-blooded Americans. On the other hand, the triad knew they were the never-caught monsters conjured up in the average guys' image of a crooked businessman. They knew, however, that their prestige, power, wealth and image in the community were the antitheses of those of a crooked businessman. Somehow, in the psyche of the public, an evil man looked evil.

These three men were well-known for their church-related activities. They were big fundraisers for veterans, police officers, firefighters and the families of men and women killed in the line of duty. Politicians sought their favor and monetary support. As Bostonians, they were well connected to the Chicago underworld and to the democratic machine, which seemed to operate without reproach. Mainly, they understood the weakness of ordinary people and how to use that weakness to their advantage. As sociopathic con artists, they had no equals.

As they descended the stairs into the banquet hall where they were being honored by the governor for their many sacrifices, they knew they had the world by the tail.

What was it that somebody would whisper into the ear of the Roman general upon entering town as the conquering hero? Number One knew there was some old wives' tale about somebody whispering into his ear, *"Remember, you are mortal,"* or some such rot, but he couldn't remember exactly what it was. *So what? Why should something stupid about the Romans enter his mind on this grand occasion?*

Cameras clicking, TV cameramen capturing every sparkling minute of the momentous event, the three heroes humbly acknowledged the adoring crowd.

Number One saw Carmen in the crowd displaying her more than adequate assets for the pleasure of all. As a piece of ass on the side, she was unbeatable. There she was entertaining his wife as if she were not the other woman. Number One saw what he wanted to see. He saw a sophisticated woman of the world who had the capacity to look like a whore or an angel. In fact, Carmen was as much a toy for the wife as for Number One.

How could Carmen not smile, being the recipient of money and pleasure from both man and wife? *What is it*, Carmen mused, *about secrets that make life so much more exciting?* Carmen couldn't decide if the gods looking down upon the grand drama were laughing or crying.

— 26 —

When Heath got word from surveillance that Ken had disappeared in his speedboat, Heath and his girlfriend, along with Chic and Suzy, were having dinner at Pandora's, their favorite steak house in the area. After a fast review of the situation, they knew that Ken could have headed east or west. He probably had not gone south through the Destin Pass. Had he gone in that direction, someone would have seen him. Unless he came back, their chances of locating him at night were nonexistent.

Chic had a bad feeling about this. Problems develop when the unexpected happens at a time when you're least prepared. Here they were at dinner, Heath having arrived in his girlfriend's car and Chic and Suzy in his Mustang. With no armored vests, assault weapons or any of the other man toys Heath kept in his official vehicle, they were basically naked. Heath had his .38 in an ankle holster and Chic was unarmed.

They both agreed, however, that they needed to pay a visit to Victor's house. If he was there, they would question him and notify him to report to the chief by nine the next morning to answer questions. If he was not there, they would snoop around the house and have an APB put out on him.

They went back to the table and Chic announced, "Ladies, Heath and I have to leave your company for a little while and do some police work. Suzy, why don't you and Mary take her car and go to my house? Heath and I will join you in a couple of hours. Suzy, why don't you pay for the meal?"

Suzy laughed. "You're an exciting date, but not that exciting. If you boys are going to leave us beautiful, young ladies by ourselves, you had better pay the bill. You might also tell me how wonderful I am."

"You know I'm an easy mark, Suzy. The boys of the Fish House Gang keep telling me I'm no fun anymore. They say all I want to do is pine over you. Is that ring through my nose that obvious?"

"Chic, you know I have a low tolerance for temptation, so you better pay that bill, give me a big kiss and then get out of here before I assault you."

Chic paid the bill, gave Suzy a big hug, a big kiss and a pat on the butt as he and Heath headed out the door.

Chic got behind the wheel of his Mustang and off they went to Victor's house.

"Here's the plan," Heath said. "We're going to see if Victor's home. If he's home, we'll order him to meet us for questioning at nine in the morning. If he gives us any lip, we'll tell him we'll be back in the morning with a warrant for his arrest. I'll tell him he's a party of interest and it's in his best interest to meet with us on a friendly basis. If necessary, I'll throw in a few threats."

"Heath, all we need to do is have you use your intimidating look and that should do the job. My guess is that he's not going to be there. He's probably with Ken somewhere."

"That's one of the reasons we're here, Chic, to confirm that he left the same time Ken did. The other is to do a general search of the outside of the house and see what we might find. Like I said, if he's not there, we'll put out an APB on him."

"We don't want to get too frisky," Chic said. "We're in my Mustang and neither one of us is dressed for action. You've got your .38 and all I have is my good looks."

"One thing for sure," Heath said, "is you're not going to scare Victor with your looks. He's a tough rascal and I don't expect him to be friendly if he's there. We both feel that something's going on and I don't think we have a lot of time. We've got Ken's house covered and we need to at least check out Victor. We'll wait a couple of hours if he's not there. It's possible that they both decided to disappear. If they do, our case is basically over. I'm going to call the chief and get some help out here as soon as possible. If we have to, we'll post them out here all night."

Victor lived in a nice house on the backside of nowhere. In typical North Florida fashion, a person could disappear in some of these out-of-the-way places and never be found. The house backed up to a small bayou that afforded access to Choctawhatchee Bay and thus to the gulf. Heath and Chic quickly established that no one was home.

"Chic, try to look in the windows and look around the house for anything of interest. I'll check out the dock area."

"Sure thing," said Chic.

Heath un-holstered his .38 and headed toward the dock area.

At the same time Heath and Chic approached his front door, Victor was approaching the entrance to the bayou behind his house. Victor had installed a high-tech security system integrated with his iPhone, with an alternative display screen in the boat. Ken allowed Victor to leave this on the boat since it had no GPS tracking devices. He had motion sensors located on the outside of his home that showed a red dot overlaid on the footprint of the house and yard. There were sensors inside and out and enough locations to accurately pinpoint the location of any intruder. Victor saw the silent alert and cut on the display. He saw two dots in the front yard, parting in opposite directions.

Victor had already pulled back on the throttle to enter the small bayou. There were no outside lights on and there was no moon, but there was enough ambient light that he could vaguely make out the dock. He was coming in noiselessly, hidden by high weeds from the view of anyone on the dock.

Victor pulled out his 9mm Glock. He kept a bullet in the chamber so he was ready for action. As he slowly and silently angled his boat to the dock, he could make out the intruder approaching the dock. Curious, a man like this nosing around at night without a flashlight. Victor could see the vague outline of a pistol in the man's hand, but he could tell by his movements that the intruder had not seen him. They were only twenty-five to thirty feet apart and Victor had the advantage. Without hesitation, Victor raised his Glock. As he fired two quick shots, the bow of the boat bumped into the dock, causing the usually accurate Victor to miss Heath's head. This error saved Heath's life.

The first shot hit a post beside Heath's head and the second grazed his right shoulder, causing him to drop his pistol. Heath fell behind a small wall, which saved him from the next two shots.

Victor was cursing himself for not aiming at the torso instead of the head, but he theorized that this intruder would have on a vest, which led him to take the head shots.

Victor was forced to either get his boat under control and get out of there or to continue fighting. To get the situation under control, he tried to bring the boat alongside the dock so he could get out and finish this guy off. He grabbed a piling with his left hand and was bringing his gun to bear on a portion of Heath's back that was exposed.

At this critical moment, Chic came from behind Victor and took a flying leap at him. Chic grabbed Victor around the neck, causing his shot to go wild.

Before Victor could react, Chic had Victor in a strangle hold and as they fell into the water Victor lost his Glock. Chic was able to pivot his body to Victor's back in a vice grip, tearing Victor between the chokehold and his strong legs wrapped around Victor's waist. Victor was a tough guy but no match for Chic. Chic was a well-trained athlete and his core muscles had been strengthened by years of breathing exercises. Chic had used this move before.

Both men were in street clothes, which made swimming difficult. Soon after hitting the water, they sank to the bottom. Victor fought like a maniac. Chic's adrenaline kicked in along with the need for fresh air. Chic's instincts and training took over and before Chic had time to process the thought, Victor's neck was broken. Chic felt Victor's body go limp and knew he was dead. Victor's dead body fell away as Chic surfaced, gasping for air. He had to check on Heath. For all he knew Heath could be dead. He could recover Victor's body after he checked on Heath.

Chic recognized that primal sense of strength and power flowing from deep within his psyche that consumed a warrior in the midst of battle. At the moment of Victor's death, Chic, in retrospect knew he was more animal than human. The beast lies close to the surface. It was this empowered beast that climbed out of the water. The monster faded as Chic directed his mind toward his injured friend.

"Heath, where are you?"

"Over here to your left, behind a little wall. He got a little piece of me, but I'll be okay." Heath cut his Mag light on so he could examine his wounds.

"I think it's a good thing you didn't have that light on," said Chic. "He would have had a better target. In fact, I don't know how he missed you from this close!"

"He was in his boat and I think it was unsteady enough that it threw his shot off. I think I was lucky to fall behind this little wall here, too. I heard the big splash. I hope that means Victor is no longer a problem."

"Yeah," said Chic. "I'm afraid to say I had to kill him. I got to him just before he was going to shoot you in the back. In the water, I didn't have time to be nice or to ask him any questions. The lizard part of my brain took over. In hand-to-hand combat, that's what happens. Now where are you hurt?"

"I got some splinters in my neck and my right shoulder hurts like hell."

Chic took the light from Heath and examined him. "Looks like a flesh wound. I have a first aid kit in the car. Stay still until I get back."

Chic cleaned and treated Heath's wounds. The bleeding was not a real problem.

"Looks like you're going to be as good as new," said Chic.

"Easy for you to say. It's not your shoulder."

"Heath, I'm going to keep your light and try to recover Victor's body. Then I'll examine his boat. If he has a GPS or phone on board, it could lead us back to wherever Ken is. Make sure we have help on the way. Otherwise sit down and rest your bones."

"Yes, Momma," replied Heath.

Chic took off his wet shoes, got down to his shorts and undershirt and dove in after Victor's body. Funny, he hadn't had time to notice until now that it was cold out there. It took Chic half an hour to recover Victor. On shore, he searched his body but found only a billfold with three hundred dollars, a driver's license, social security card and Bank of America credit card—nothing meaningful in this case. Chic then searched the boat. No radio, no GPS, no charts and nothing that would give him a hint to Ken's whereabouts.

Victor's security system was still on. Heath's location was clearly marked on the screen. Chic carefully checked the monitor and it became apparent there was no history of any kind kept on the monitor and certainly no records as to GPS locations.

Chic checked Victor's body for a cell phone, but there was no cell phone or even radio on Victor or his boat. His gun was also missing.

The main thing of interest to Chic was the absence of the radio and GPS and charts of any kind. It was obvious to Chic that the boat had been stripped of any devices that would lead them back to Ken. Chic was certain at this point that Ken was gone. *Was Victor supposed to be with him?*

Chic concluded that whatever operation Ken was involved with in this area was done and over with. Everybody who knew anything was dead, except for Ken, who was gone. At this point, law enforcement would have no further interest in the big picture, if in fact there was a big picture.

When the sun comes up, they'd search the place again and put some divers out to see what they could find in the water. Then they'd search Victor's house, but Chic doubted there would be anything in the house with any relevance.

Help showed up by the time Chic completed his search of the boat and the recovery of Victor's body.

Chic called Suzy and brought her up to date on the events of the night. "Doll, I'll see you first thing in the morning. I'm sure I'll be up all night filling out forms and reports. You know how it is when you kill somebody." Around seven-thirty a.m., Chic was finally released to go home.

Forty miles to the east, a small helicopter made its way to a freighter sailing sixty miles off the coast of Destin, headed to Vera Cruz, Mexico. Ken looked out the window upon a glorious day, cool and bright. The pure white sand gave the illusion of snow on a cold day. Happy to be leaving a messy situation, thrilled to be alive and headed for an exciting life in international finance, Ken was in a rare state of elation.

With his knowledge of the corporate daisy chain, his understanding of money laundering and his hands on unlimited cash, he couldn't wait to exercise the power that was his. Not alone, he knew, but his nonetheless. Ken knew that this ability to act as quarterback and the management of the religious corporations, which was the basic tool he used to launder money, would keep him alive and well in the company.

His elation and feeling of unlimited power was a little tarnished in his mind by the image of Chic. Every man, great or small, has his nemesis. Chic was his. Totally unmoved by all the man toys and the power brought by wealth, Chic stood as his antithesis. *Well,* Ken thought, smiling to himself, *I hope he gets the note I left for him in the safe.*

— 27 —

Chic was able to talk the police into searching Ken's house and office and Victor's house and office. The information shed light on many of the corporate names, which turned out to be legitimate businesses. The bottom line was that there was nothing left of the businesses operated by Ken. All his assets were either leased or heavily mortgaged. The creditors had already moved in for the kill. No valuable crumbs were left behind.

Chic was surprised that Ken was carrying a heavy debt load. Chic could see no evidence that the creditors were bogus, although it was possible. There was no way he could chase that red herring. He had to conclude, however, that the kind of debt Ken owed was totally inconsistent with the image Ken portrayed. Based on what Chic knew about Ken's operation, he was convinced that the debt was essentially bogus. It was also very effective in probably more ways than he could comprehend. Chic was careful to preserve the names of the creditors.

It was clear that Ken had carefully planned his exit, although in some ways it was as if he left in the middle of a hot meal, still steaming. Chic was impressed with the methodical way Ken had stripped his home and business of anything meaningful to his investigation. Ken's vault at his home was a jewel. Essentially, they would not have found it had Ken not left all the safes open.

The vault was so well concealed that you would have to have a set of the plans to realize there was some unaccounted for space in the house. The main safe was totally empty except for an envelope containing one sheet of paper and addressed to "Chic Sparks." Inside was the following handwritten note:

Dear Chic:

I couldn't leave without thanking you for the heads-up advice. I just wanted you to know that I am mindful that you and I have made different choices in life. I have gone for money, power and security. You have chosen a life not controlled by lust, greed and the pursuit of man toys. I admire your choices but am consumed by mine. We answer to different masters.

I will miss the repartee with the Fish House Gang.

Your Friend,

Ken

The divers recovered Victor's Glock but nothing important to Chic's investigation. Chic took the time and energy to detail all the corporation names he could locate, as well as all individual names he could find. The information filled several compact discs. It would take Chic some time to analyze it all. It looked like a dead-end job and he really didn't have the time, energy and motivation to tackle this project. All the files went to storage and Chic shut it out of his mind as history.

To Chic, the information on the disc was part of his stock in trade. He didn't know how or when, but his gut told him that he would see this beast again. He had cut off a couple of tentacles, but the big octopus remained intact.

Suzy and Chic lay in their lounge chairs by the pool on the deck of the Holland American cruise ship, baking in the bright sun. They were on their way to Martinique and other southern Caribbean islands, holding hands like two teenagers.

"You know, Chic, I've never taken a cruise before and it's just wonderful. After this, you might be able to get me on a sailboat."

"Babe, I'm convinced you would make a wonderful sailor. When we get back, I'll give you a few lessons and we'll join a race team at the Fort Walton Yacht Club. I don't want to get too fresh out here in public, Suzy, but the boys at the Fish House Gang are right about me. I'm convinced that you're capable of doing about anything you set your mind to. I'm just a little puppy dog waiting for a pat on the head."

Suzy leaned over and gave Chic a kiss and a hug, sensual enough to send the old man's heart into fibrillation.

"Quit teasing me, Chic. What do you want me to do? Admit that the ring is in my nose, not yours?" Suzy leaned back and looked Chic square in the eyes. "Chic, I don't want to get too serious out here beside the pool, but you know you saved my life in many ways. You saved me from myself and in reality saved me from that killer. Then you introduced me to Christ, who saved my soul. What's more, the first time I saw you, you took my heart. So if I don't ever get the words out this way again, thanks."

"Since we're confessing, I have to admit that you got my heart the first time I met you coming out of your class. I'll tell you I feel blessed to be with you. I don't want to sound like some misguided romantic, but I find it most amazing that we can actually read each other without saying a word. I guess that's what they mean by soul mates."

"That's sweet, Chic. I have to tell you that you're a romantic and I love you. Don't ever stop being a romantic. Chic, do you see that old couple up on the next level above the pool? They've been watching us for a while now and they look at each other like two turtle doves. I hope that when we get old, we'll still be as happy together as they are. It's inspiring to me to believe that you can still be happy and as attracted to each other as they obviously are at their age."

"Babe, I think that we've inspired them as much as they've inspired us. I hate to spoil the mood, but I can't help but think about Ken and that note he left me."

"That was a weird note and message from a crook and a killer. What do you think he meant?"

"Ken was a rascal, a crook, a dishonest businessman and probably a killer. He was also my friend. Ken understood that he reached a time in his life when he had to make a decision. His decision was to commit to the path of seeking wealth, power and in his mind, security. He saw in me the other path. He admitted that he would not abandon the path he was on. The tragedy of Goethe's *Faust* was that he sold his soul to the devil. Ken essentially is letting me know that he made the same decision. We all reach that point in life when we have to decide which way we're going. Unlike Ken, you chose life."

"Ken was in so deep that he felt he couldn't get out," Suzy said.

"I'm sure that's the way he felt, but even the thief on the cross had time to save his soul. I would like to think that Ken had time to save his soul, but I have the distinct feeling that his number has been called."

— 28 —

Ken was elated that he was able to leave the cabin and get to the freighter without incident. Too bad about Victor. Normally Victor was a rational guy, one who didn't take any unnecessary chances. Why he felt it was necessary to make that last trip back home was, well, pretty stupid according to Ken. Perhaps he should have put his foot down and refused to let Victor return home. All Ken knew at this point was that Victor had not returned and he was on his own. It would be unfortunate if he were arrested by the sheriff, but Victor was tough enough to keep his mouth shut. Was it possible that Victor was driven by some deep-seated death wish? Ken was convinced that more people have this malady than one would believe. Some things in life were simply counter intuitive.

Ken was certain that by now Boston was aware that Victor had not made it back to the cabin and that Victor had been left behind. George would be on top of the situation. He would be able to handle what was left of the business in the Panhandle. Ken had no illusion about Victor's future. He was a dead man walking. Ken was satisfied that Victor was aware of his limited longevity. As was Ken's custom, Victor's existence was wiped from his conscious mind as though Victor never existed. Ken was rather proud of his unique ability to simply close off a period of time or a person from his mind when they became useless to his future endeavors. Ken was therefore able to move forward without the prior friendships. Victor had made a bone-headed decision and was no longer relevant to Ken's business. Boston would elevate George to take over the loan business and probably the gold-buying business. George would continue to serve his function with the cartel in the drug business. None of that was relevant to Ken at this time, so he was now free to direct all his energies toward his future in Belize with no baggage from the past.

Ken left his room on the freighter and settled down in the mess hall for a morning snack of orange juice, coffee and a divine sausage biscuit. He would have to compliment the captain on his room and the food on board. Being at sea in any kind of sea-worthy vessel was the type of experience that lifted his spirits. He pondered those poor souls who do not feel at home at sea. Many of them felt cramped, confined, got seasick and were just generally miserable at sea. *What pussies!*

Today the Gulf of Mexico was on its best behavior. Gentle waves, gentle breeze, nice temperature, bright sun—why even the distant oil platforms added to the pleasure of the moment. A world entirely free of the strictures of land-based society. Here, given a few days existing on a time scale truly dictated by the movements of the sun's path through its course in the sky, one's bodily systems were more closely attuned to nature's rhythm. Only a sailor understands that noon on the clock doesn't correspond to high noon at one's exact location on land or at sea. Birds follow the rising sun, noon sun and setting sun based on its location in the sky, not the movement of a clock. *Surely,* thought Ken, *it was intended for man to follow the natural order of the universe rather than artificial dictates of time divided into segments ticked off by a clock.*

Ken's mind, free of land-based worries, probed the crevices and dark corners of his mind. Thus levitated of burdens, he understood that though he was cultured, civilized and fully capable of moving within normal society, he was nonetheless part of the animal kingdom. *Man did descend from the animal kingdom, didn't they?* Ken recognized the beast within himself. He was comfortable with that beast. *Man, in truth, was nothing more than a cultivated beast with enough intellect for reflective thinking.* Perhaps man has a soul. Ken had no opinion on that. *When you tear away all the veneer from man, separate him from his antiseptic cocoon, expose him to cold or extreme heat, make him forage for food and isolate him from his support system, a highly intelligent beast emerges. Take that same individual and mix him with a mob of similarly deprived individuals and you get a mob of intelligent, destructive human gorillas. In other words, man reduced to his core level.*

Ken laughed at himself for such thoughts. More a sneer than a laugh. Despite Ken's sociopath tendencies, he was capable of reflective thinking and was a good student of human nature and behavior. Ken's problem was that he had no sense of right and wrong and no guilt to burden him down. Truth for Ken was at best an abstract vision, a mirage, something to be molded as a tool. Ken could discern the weakness of any poor, trusting soul and in short order they would trust him with their sister.

A religious person would recognize Ken as being possessed by that same devil that tempted Christ to abuse his power as God incarnate. The devil first appears with a gift of honey.

Captain Bill Rumsey walked into the mess hall, went over to Ken, put his hand on Ken's shoulder and said, "You don't mind if I interrupt your deep contemplation, do you?"

Captain Rumsey was a mercurial man, well dressed in a starched uniform with sharp creases and shoes highly polished. At five feet eight inches tall, one hundred sixty five pounds, he presented the image of the quintessential sea captain—professional to the core.

Ken was actually startled. He realized that he probably looked like a monk in deep prayer, sitting there alone, staring out with a blank look on his face toward the sea and the bow of the freighter as it rocked into the crest of each wave.

"No, no, Bill, have a seat. I planned to come to tell you that your cook is excellent. If I ever take another trip on a freighter, I'm going to give you a call."

"How is your room?"

"The room is great. This is actually a good way to travel if you're not in a hurry."

"Well, Ken, I've been told by other people that this is the way to go, unless you want to see the big productions they have on the cruise ships. It's common for us to have four to five guests on the boat. This trip, you're it. Generally speaking, the kinds of people who travel by freighter are regulars. A lot of them have had some long-time connection to the sea. The merchant marine types, for example, like to travel this way. I understand that you're going to get off in Vera Cruz. We had hoped that you were going to stay on until Belize."

"That was my original plan, but I've decided to get on my sail boat, the *Amadee* and make the last leg on her. It's been awhile since I've had a chance to get on the *Amadee* for an extended trip."

"I've heard that the Amel is a great sailboat. I understand you have a fifty-three-foot Maramu, is that right?"

"Yes. It's a great boat. It is built for the North Sea. With twenty-knots of wind and five- or six-foot waves, the *Amadee* begins to settle into its groove. I haven't been in a full-blown hurricane with her, but I've sailed in some tough gale force winds in the Gulf of Mexico. As you know, Captain, that's sort of like being stuck in a washing machine."

"Yes, indeed, you're right about that, Ken. The Gulf of Mexico is a nasty sea of confused wave patterns. That's because it's an enclosed bowl with narrow exits between Cuba and Mexico and between Cuba and Key West. The Gulf Stream flowing into that bowl is responsible for that confused pattern, combined of course with the many northerlies coming from North America."

"Captain Bill, today is not one of those rough days. Can't ask for any better."

"Well, I'll tell you what, Ken, if you keep a close lookout you'll be able to see a lot of sea creatures today. You can't really see them except on calm days. If you look close you might even see a few humpback whales. We saw an entire pod yesterday. If you like, we'll go take a look when I finish my coffee."

"Good deal, Captain. I would like to do that."

"So tell me more about the *Amadee*, Ken. Is it everything they say?"

"You bet. When you buy an Amel in America, they have to sail the boat from La Rochelle in the Bay of Biscay, France, to America. When you step on board it has already been tested. It's a ketch rig, low aspect. Basically, it is a working boat, built for cruising. It's built for white-water sailing. You can control the sails from the cockpit with toggle switches. Very convenient in heavy weather and when shorthanded. Everywhere you move on the boat there's a convenient handhold. In a good wind, except when the wind is on your nose, you can get full speed with the one hundred fifty degree genoa and mizzenmast. This allows the boat to sail in a pretty flat posture. Then we have a water maker, a generator, adequate refrigeration, air conditioning, every navigation tool you can put on a boat this size, a super TV and all the communication devices you could hope for. Frankly, I'd rather live on the *Amadee* than any place I've ever lived. Maybe I will someday."

"Tell you what, Ken. When I retire in a couple of years, I may give you a call and volunteer my services for any upcoming trips you have planned."

"Captain, that's a deal. Call me. Let us take our coffee out on the bridge and see if we can see any whales."

It could have been the wonderful weather, the food or just the elation from escaping Florida before he could be arrested that kept Ken in high spirits for the three days he was on the freighter. When they arrived at Vera Cruz, Captain Rumsey and Ken made some general plans to work on a cruise in a year or so, shook hands and parted to complete their separate tasks for the day.

Captain Bart Hayes, captain of the *Amadee*, was waiting for Ken in the dingy which was tied up at the dock in the commercial ship area. Bart was waving his hand to get Ken's attention. The two made contact and Ken quickly boarded the dingy. Within thirty minutes Ken was aboard the *Amadee* and as was his custom took charge as captain. The *Amadee* was made ready and they motored away from the dock area. After about twenty-five miles, the wind picked up, so Ken engaged the headsail and mizzenmast. The boat was making seven knots as it headed east-southeast toward Ciudad del Carmen, which was about a day and a half sail or approximately thirty-six hours away. They planned to spend a day there and then head toward Isla Mujeres, about a three or four day trip. They would spend a couple of days in the Cancun area and then head to Belize.

Ken placed the boat on autopilot so he could go below and speak with the crew. Captain Hayes was at the navigation and chart table, working out the course as well as their ETA. They would try to enter ports during daylight hours.

The crew, Doug and Bo-Bo, were busy at their normal tasks. Doug was the cook and chief bottle washer. Bo-Bo was in charge of maintenance. Both men had to pull watch duty, act as sailors and were tasked with keeping the boat clean and shiny.

By comparison to the captain and crew of the freighter, Ken couldn't help but notice that Captain Hayes, Doug and Bo-Bo looked more like rejects from the cast of *Pirates of the Caribbean*. Captain Hayes had a dark complexion, a mass of black hair, a hairy chest, usually a two-day-old beard and a nasty attitude. To his credit, he did a bang-up job as the captain of *Amadee*.

Doug, the cook, well, he looked like a cook on a fishing boat. Generally unkempt with a small frame of five feet seven inches, one hundred fifty pounds, he couldn't scare anybody. His saving grace was that he never ran short of tall tales and could generally entertain everybody at night.

Bo-Bo was what you would call the deck ape. He had a shaved head, a round face with a pleasant smile and a personality that hid the true nature of the dangerous beast underneath. Bo-Bo had no problem at six feet, two hundred forty pounds, with handling all the heavy work on board.

The crew had known Ken for a good while and actually liked him. He never abused them as long as they did their jobs. They especially liked the fact that Ken was so busy that he didn't use the boat very often. This meant that the crew normally had the boat to themselves. What a deal: free room and board, good pay and the right to use this million-dollar boat to impress the women. A man couldn't ask for any better.

"What's for supper, Doug?"

"Boss, I've got us some fresh lobster. We'll have that along with corn on the cob, great salad and top it off with my famous bread pudding. If you ever get a chance to order your last meal, this is it."

"I'll make a point to remember that, Doug."

After the group left Ciudad del Carmen, they decided to pass Merida and head directly to Cancun. The gulf was a little choppy and the wind a little more in your face, but nothing that would cause the *Amadee* any problems. The waves in the gulf had a tendency to develop a sharp peak with a short distance between crests. The main problem was that you had to hold on. When you came off the crest of the wave into the trough you could easily be dropping ten feet. If you weren't holding on you could find yourself dropping butt-first from the headliner in the cabin. Everybody aboard had busted their butt at one time or another, so no one had to remind them to hold on.

As Ken was enjoying himself on the *Amadee*, he didn't know that Chic and Suzy were boarding a cruise ship in Fort Lauderdale. Nor did he know an encrypted call was being placed to Captain Bart. Nor could Chic have known that at the same time he and Suzy were boarding their cruise ship in Fort Lauderdale, Ken was the subject of that encrypted phone call.

"Captain Hayes, this is Number One. Is the fish food aboard?"

"Yes, sir," said the captain. "We plan on slipping him a sedative at supper that will knock him out cold."

"Excellent. When you get off Cantoy Island, feed the fish." Number One signed off with no further contact.

On Chic and Suzy's first night at sea, Ken was dispatched by the captain of the *Amadee* to contribute his body to the sea creatures off Cantoy Island which lay at the northeastern tip of the Yucatan.

Because the crew really liked Ken they decided to complete this assignment as humanely as possible. After Captain Bart Hayes pronounced a few words consistent with one who believed in neither God nor the afterlife, Ken was injected with a lethal dose of sedatives. When Ken's soul left his body for his appointed day of judgment, the crew carefully prepared his body for disbursement as seafood.

Located north of Cancun in the Gulf Stream is a deep drop-off running north- northeast. Each night, fishing boats by the hundreds line up on this deep-water bank to harvest the treasure of the sea. Ken would perhaps find some satisfaction that while his soul was with his father, the devil, his body would serve the useful purpose of feeding the fish that would eventually grace someone's table. It is well known that demons devour their own.

As Ken's body descended into Davy Jones's Locker, a strange pink glow emanated from the eastern sky. A chilled breeze whipped over the sailors' necks emptying their body from warmth. As though engulfed in the twilight zone, the *Amadee* sailors in symphonic harmony shook as an evil spirit engulfed their very souls. From some dark place in the pit of their bellies, they understood they had crossed a threshold into hell itself.

The beast that lies within smiled and recognized the pink sky as a smile of approval from Father Devil himself. The principalities and powers that be rose up in that eternal conflict between good and evil. Tonight - evil rode a transient tide of victory - rising until dissipated by the hand of Father God.

CPSIA information can be obtained
at www.ICGtesting.com
Printed in the USA
JSHW021243260723
45234JS00003BA/12

9 781480 800748